THE BRIDGE OF WHISPERS

KRISTIN BUTCHER

CP | CRWTH PRESS

Library and Archives Canada Cataloguing in Publication

Title: The bridge of whispers / Kristin Butcher.
Names: Butcher, Kristin, 1951- author.
Description: Series statement: Seer trilogy ; book II
Identifiers: Canadiana (print) 2021022391X | Canadiana (ebook) 20210223936 | ISBN 9781989724118 (softcover) | ISBN 9781989724132 (EPUB)
Classification: LCC PS8553.U6972 B75 2021 | DDC jC813/.54—dc23

Cover and interior design by Julia Breese
Copy edited by Laura Langston
Proofread by Audrey McClellan

Crwth Press gratefully acknowledges the support of the Province of British Columbia through the British Columbia Arts Council.

Crwth Press
#204 – 2320 Woodland Drive
Vancouver, BC V5N 3P2
www.crwth.ca

Printed and bound in Canada.

BRIDGE OF WHISPERS MAP
KING'S CASTLE
EASTERN SEA
CASTLE CARRICK
VILLAGE
FERGUS'S FARM
BRIDGE OF WHISPERS
THE RUIN
SOUTHERN SEA
VILLAGE

Chapter 1

Everyone in the Ruin was sleeping—everyone but Maeve. She lay still and listened to Enda's even breathing beside her and the fitful snores of Nora across the room. A hint of daylight pushed through the gaps of the shutters. It was time.

Maeve slid out from under the coverlet. Her toes curled away from the cold stone floor, and she had to will herself to place her foot down. For a moment she considered diving back into her warm bed. She reached for her mantle and wrapped it around herself. Then she tiptoed to the door, tugged on her boots and dragged the door open enough to slip through.

She felt like a thief. But she was only stealing a few moments alone with the morning. Nothing more.

Outside she lifted her face to the sky and inhaled. Brisk winter air filled her lungs, and her body tingled with the freshness of it. Maeve watched each expelled breath billow forth in a small cloud, as if she were a dragon blowing smoke. She hugged her mantle tighter and started across the lea. The grass was brittle with frost and crunched beneath her boots.

Glancing behind her, she saw the stone walls of the Ruin in silhouette against the awakening sky—tall and angular here, rounded there, ragged and crumbling everywhere. No one knew who had built it. It had been abandoned long ago and reclaimed by nature. It was a maze of grassy trenches and stacked stones—all covered with ivy. Its pathways criss-crossed to create numerous small enclosed spaces. The Druids had adopted it as their own, adding doors and shutters and roofing the sleeping quarters. The result was exactly right.

Maeve still couldn't believe her good fortune. Mere months ago she'd been a blacksmith's daughter. Her parents and sister had thought her strange and useless. The village folk said she was simple. And then last summer a wise old Druid had told her she possessed the gift of sight and offered to take her on as his apprentice.

That had changed everything. She was still a blacksmith's daughter, but now she lived among the Druids and her life was as different as it could be. She'd been called upon to interpret the dreams of the Great King, and she had exposed a plot to take control of the kingdom. She was no longer the useless simple girl she'd once been.

She lowered herself onto a stone bench. The cold seeped through her mantle and numbed her legs, but she barely noticed. She turned her gaze toward the eastern horizon and waited for the sun to show itself.

"Good morning."

"Declan!" She beamed. "I thought I was the only one awake."

He sat down beside her and reached for her hand. "You're ice cold."

She laughed. "It's winter. Look. The sun is coming."

Together they watched as the sky blushed pink and then faded to rose, giving way to sparks of blinding light that shot up from the horizon in brilliant flashes. The sun gradually pulled itself up and flooded the sky with a deep orange hue. Morning had arrived.

"The sunrise is always so beautiful," she said. "I'm already looking forward to the next one."

Declan chuckled. "Then you must hate cloudy mornings."

"I do!" she declared. "It's as if the sun has sneaked into the sky."

"Then you must hold the memory of sunrises such as this in your mind so that you can see them again when it's overcast."

"Just as you bards memorize stories?" Maeve teased.

"Something like that."

A series of thuds and thumps started up behind them, and they turned to see Cara pulling logs from the woodpile for the morning fire.

"And the day begins." Declan slapped his thighs.

"I hope yours is a good one, Maeve." Then, trotting back toward the Ruin, he called, "Cara, let me help you."

As Maeve watched him go, contentment warmed her. Not only did she have a home with the Druids, she had a special friend in Declan. They had an understanding—friendship for now, but perhaps more in the future.

Maeve frowned. Was that possible? Declan was a Druid, but she was not. Did that mean friends was all they could ever be?

She broached the subject to Enda as they cleared away the morning meal. Though Enda was nearly twice Maeve's age, the two had become fast friends.

"Why do Druids live separately from other people?" she asked.

Enda stopped gathering the wooden platters from the long table and pushed the bench in with her knee. "I suppose it's because of what we do. Most folk are farmers, tinkers, weavers and such. But Druids walk a different path. We are teachers, musicians, bards, healers. People value our knowledge and skills, but they are wary of us." She shrugged. "So the decision to remain apart from other folk is made for us. We merely oblige." She went back to clearing the table.

"Do Druids ever marry other folk?"

"Hmm." Enda considered Maeve's question. "There's no law against it that I know of, but I can't say I've ever heard of it happening."

Maeve hesitated before asking her next question. "Do other common folk like me live among Druids?"

Once more Enda paused in her work. "Sometimes a person who is not a Druid will show promise for teaching or healing and will be taken on as an apprentice. But I've never heard of such a thing with diviners. Only Druids possess the gift of sight. At least that's what I thought before you came along. Bradan says you are as gifted a seer as ever he's met. But you are not a Druid."

Maeve lowered her voice. "Do the others at the Ruin know that?"

Enda shook her head. "As far as I know, the subject hasn't come up."

"It's just that I … I … " Maeve stammered. "Everyone is so kind. I can't help wondering if they would be as friendly if they knew I wasn't one of them."

There it was—her old fear of not belonging. Despite the kindness the Druids had shown her since she'd been living among them, Maeve still felt like an outsider.

"Oh, pish posh. That makes no difference," Enda declared. "You mightn't be a Druid by birth, but you should be. There's no one can deny that, so don't be worrying your head about it. You are loved because of who you are—a sweet and generous soul." She pointed to the fire. "Although you do need practice washing pots. And since the water has come to the boil, I suggest you get on with it."

After the morning meal, Maeve usually had lessons with Bradan. But since he had other business to tend to this day, she saw her chance to explore the nearby woods. Though she had lived at the Ruin for nearly two weeks, she hadn't had time to get to know the area.

The forest swallowed her up the instant she stepped into the trees. The magic of it burrowed beneath her skin and curled around her bones. Every fibre of her being prickled with energy. It was a wonder sparks didn't fly from her fingertips.

She went where her feet took her as if the forest was guiding her. Pine needles, decaying leaves and sodden wood chips silenced her footfalls. She picked her way around the trees, absently running her hands over the bark, her fingers bumping in and out of the rough grooves and eventually through a sluggish rivulet of pitch. She scooped up a handful of dirt to clear away the stickiness. As she rubbed the sandy earth over her fingers, she found herself staring at a bead of dew fattening on the end of a branch. She closed her eyes and took the earthy woodland essence into her lungs.

That's when she heard water tumbling over rocks. She quickly scrubbed the remaining pitch from her hand and followed the sound to the banks of a small brook. The stream was shallow and narrow, though not so narrow that she could hop to the opposite bank. Maeve watched the water ripple over and around the rocks, polishing them with wetness. There was a peacefulness about it that urged her to linger, but as she looked for a place to sit, a breeze hurried past the trees behind her and one of the boughs brushed her neck.

Maeve spun around. "What?" She thought she'd heard someone speak. "Who's there?"

But there was no response, and though she stared long into the trees, she saw nothing unusual.

She shook her head. Her mind was playing tricks on her. Despite months of lessons aimed at teaching her how to manage her gift, Maeve was still sometimes plagued by bizarre imaginings. She made a mental note to ask Bradan if this happened to all seers or if it was simply *her* mind that was unruly.

She pushed the notion aside. She should continue her explorations. She looked upstream and down, wondering which way to go. Then, lifting the hem of her robe, she continued following the flow of water. This choice offered no more promise than the other but something pulled her this way.

She came to a place where the water abandoned its leisurely course and rushed at the rocks blocking its way, spewing white foam as it crashed into them. Peering downstream, Maeve saw the reason for the change in the water's nature. Directly ahead was a small waterfall, pulling the stream to it and dragging it over the edge.

Buffeted this way and that, the water thrashed angrily as it hurtled down the drop into a pool below. Maeve watched the churning foam ripple away and settle into stillness. Not complete stillness, for the water continued moving, albeit lazily now. She looked toward the place where the pool narrowed back into a stream and hurried on its way again.

Maeve caught her breath. A stone bridge crossed the stream. And standing in the middle of it was a woman. Her back was to Maeve, so all she could see was the woman's torso and a shock of copper curls trailing to her waist. Without realizing, Maeve twisted a tendril of her own hair around her finger.

"Hello!" She clambered over the stones to get to the bridge. But she was moving with too much haste and not enough care, and she slipped, banging her knee on a large rock.

When she looked back the woman was gone.

Wincing and rubbing her bruised knee, Maeve carried on to the bridge. Crossing over to the other bank, she called out several times, but there was no reply. The red-haired woman had disappeared.

Maeve wondered who she was. Not a Druid from the Ruin. Maeve would have remembered her. One didn't see hair that colour every day. She must be a villager. But what was she doing in the forest? And why had she run away?

Maeve was still puzzling over the matter when she returned to the Ruin. Spying Enda and Nora by the cooking fire, she made her way to them.

"What have you been up to this day?" Nora asked as she slid chopped turnips and carrots into the soup pot.

"I went for a walk in the forest."

Enda snorted. "Never have I known anyone who spends as much time in the woods as you."

Maeve lowered her eyes. "It's peaceful there."

Nora patted her hand. "It surely is." She glared at her daughter. "Mostly because it's free of squawking birds."

Enda sniffed. "I'm not saying anything that isn't true. Maeve is a creature of the forest. I didn't say it was a bad thing. Don't be scowling at me, Mother."

Nora turned to Maeve. "So what did you find there, lass?"

"A lovely little stream." Maeve brightened at the memory. "And a bridge spanning it. I crossed over, but there was no trail. What's on the other side?"

Nora shook her head. "Nothing that I know of."

"So why is there a bridge?"

"Perhaps it was built by hunters," Enda suggested. "It would be easier to haul a stag over a bridge than through a stream."

"Does the bridge have a name?"

"It does," Nora replied. "It is called the Bridge of Whispers."

"The Bridge of Whispers," Maeve murmured. "That's beautiful. Do people often go there?"

"Children at play I imagine, but no one else that I'm aware. There's naught to draw a body to it. I haven't set eyes on the place since I was a girl younger than you."

Maeve turned to her friend. "Do you ever go there, Enda?"

"Sometimes—when I'm foraging for burdock root. It likes to grow on the banks. But I can't recall seeing anyone there." Her rosy round face split into a grin. "Though I suspect now that you've discovered it, that will change."

Maeve wanted to ask about the red-haired woman she'd seen, but she decided against it. The woman had disappeared so quickly and completely, Maeve wasn't sure she'd been real. She didn't want Enda and Nora to think she was losing her wits, so it was best to keep the young woman to herself. If she were real, she would show herself again.

Chapter 2

The next morning Maeve found Bradan in his usual spot in a copse of stately oak trees. He was sitting on a log beneath a web of frosted branches—a sparkling arch of winter lace against the blue sky. Even from a distance Maeve could tell he was deep in thought. She wondered what weighty matters he was pondering. She was envious. Her own thoughts skittered from one frivolous notion to the next. And though she diligently worked at the mind-taming tasks Bradan set for her, they seemed to have little effect. It was hard to believe she would ever control what went on in her head.

"Good morning," she called and hurried to join him.

Bradan's eyes glittered and the corners of his mouth twitched. "A good morning it is indeed. Bracing, but that gets the old blood moving." He rubbed his hands together and peered up into the branches of the trees. "It won't be long before these trees fatten with buds. New life—is there anything better?"

As Maeve followed his gaze skyward, she thought about her sister. Deirdre was expecting her first child, and it seemed fitting to Maeve that it should be born in spring along with the other miracles of nature. Even more wonderful was that Deirdre had asked Maeve to be with her.

Bradan gestured to the tree stump across from him. "Tell me what you did yesterday while I was in the village," he said once she was seated.

"I went into the forest."

He nodded. "Was it as you expected?" Before Maeve could reply, he chuckled. "No need to answer, child. You have a look about you that says everything that needs saying. Would that I could connect with you as the forest does."

Maeve reached across the space separating them and covered his old gnarled hand with her youthful one. "Oh, but you do, Bradan," she said. "I couldn't ask for a better teacher. You make me think about things I've never considered. I don't always understand them," she confessed, "but I'm certain one day they'll make sense. And when I'm old, I'll be as knowing and wise as you."

Bradan's shoulders shook with silent laughter. "Don't be in too much of a hurry for that," he said. "Old age comes quicker than you know, and wisdom doesn't always arrive with it. Nevertheless, we shall make that our goal." He cleared his throat. "Let us begin with your walk through the forest yesterday. What did you learn?"

"There's a lovely stream running through it.

I could almost imagine it was talking to me." She rubbed her bruised knee. "Also the rocky banks are slippery and one needs to walk them with care."

Bradan nodded. "Yes, experience can be an uncomfortable—though effective—teacher."

"Well, I won't try to run on those rocks again, that's for certain," Maeve replied. "I also discovered a bridge, which seems strange. The stream is so narrow it hardly needs a bridge, especially one that doesn't lead anywhere."

Bradan nodded and a faraway look came over him. "The Bridge of Whispers," he murmured.

"Yes," Maeve said. "Why is it called that?" When Bradan didn't reply, she repeated her question. When he still didn't answer, she called his name.

The old man pulled himself from his reverie. "I'm sorry," he said. "My thoughts were wandering. One of the nuisances of old age." He forced a smile. He was trying to make a joke, but Maeve thought he looked unsettled. He shook his head as if trying to bring the world back into focus. "Did you ask me something?"

"I asked if you knew how the bridge got its name."

He turned her question back on her. "How do *you* think the bridge came to be named?"

Inwardly Maeve groaned. The old Druid rarely gave her a straight answer, which generally meant a lesson of some sort was on its way. Feeling herself slide into a sour mood, she scowled.

"I don't know." And then, because she knew she had to at least attempt a reply, she added, "Perhaps the breeze blowing through the trees sounds like whispers. Or maybe people go there to share secrets. Can't you just tell me?"

Bradan pulled back and regarded her with raised eyebrows. "It is of little value to accept my word on things out of hand," he said. "You need to work them out for yourself."

"Why?" she demanded irritably. "We could save so much time if you just told me."

"That would be false economy."

"Why?"

"Because tomorrow you will have forgotten it. When you discover the answer yourself, the meaning will stay with you."

"Perhaps that's how it is for you," Maeve argued. "It makes no sense to make me hunt for an answer that *you* already know. It's like insisting I weave a basket to collect apples when there's a perfectly good basket already made."

Bradan regarded her sternly. "If the goal is to gather apples, any basket will do. However, if the goal is to master basket weaving, it would be best to attempt the task yourself."

Maeve opened her mouth to protest. Bradan cut her off. "You haven't given any thought to what I've said, yet you are determined to disagree." He tapped his head. "You must learn to speak less and think more." Before she could reply, he added, "For today's lesson you will return to the bridge and observe the area. When you have determined how the bridge got its name, you may return. Do you understand?"

Maeve scowled and nodded.

"Good." Bradan flapped his hand at her. "Then you'd best get started."

As Maeve made her way to the stream, she pondered the task Bradan had set for her. Given the entire day to think about things, she could surely come up with a few explanations for the name of the bridge. But how was she to know which—if any—was correct? For all she knew, Bradan didn't know the answer. He hadn't said he did. What if this task was nothing more than an exercise to stretch her thinking muscles? Or perhaps he wanted to keep her busy so he could rest. Maeve kicked a stone. His reason didn't matter. She still had to do as he said.

At the foot of the bridge she stopped and listened. The air was still. The only sounds were birds chirping and the stream rippling over rocks, and neither of those resembled whispers.

She walked among the trees, searching for some sort of wind tunnel. The air rushing through might sound like whispers. Round and round the trees she tramped, standing on her toes, then hunkering down, all the while listening as hard as she could. But there was not so much as the thump of a fallen pine cone.

She needed to investigate the bridge itself. Perhaps the space between the walls acted as a wind tunnel. Maeve knelt down at one end and waited for air to stream past. But there was nothing. She crossed over and did the same on the other side. The result was no different. She examined the bridge's surface, looking for cracks or holes that might allow air to whisper on its way through, but the little bridge was as solid as if it had been chiselled from a single block of stone. She lay on the bridge, hoping that might reveal something, but, of course, it didn't. She got back to her feet and pulled her mantle tightly around her, for the stone was cold.

Why was this called the Bridge of Whispers? Bradan spoke as if the answer could be found here. People might have come for clandestine meetings, but that was only a guess. The only sensible explanation was that when air moved past the bridge, it sounded like whispers. But there had to be wind for that. She gazed up into the trees. They were as still as stones.

She would have to wait. Looking for a sunny place to sit, she pulled a crust of bread and a chunk of cheese from the pocket of her robe. She was glad she'd brought food because this had the makings of a long day.

All afternoon she stared at the heavy branches of the evergreens and waited for wind to riffle them and whisper to her. But even when shadows grew long, the air remained stubbornly still. Maeve stood and stretched. If she didn't start back to the Ruin soon, it would be dark before she got there. Bradan had told her she must discover the reason for the bridge's name before she returned, but surely he didn't mean for her to stay in the forest all night.

Hoping the bridge might yet tell her something, she walked onto it and stared over the stone wall into the stream. Her image stared back, rippling with the water.

While she watched, her image became two, one slightly behind the other. That was strange. She frowned and stared harder into the stream. There were definitely two of her—two slender girls with copper curls spilling over their shoulders.

Maeve was gazing at herself—and yet she wasn't. When she raised a hand to her hair, but the reflection of the second girl did not, she knew she was seeing two people.

She whirled around.

No one was there. She turned back to the water. The only face returning her gaze was her own. Maeve's heart began to beat faster.

The red-haired woman had been behind her. She was sure of it. This was the second time she'd seen her—and the second time she'd vanished. Flesh-and-blood people didn't do that.

For many minutes she stayed on the bridge, waiting for the young woman to reappear. But she didn't. As Maeve's own reflection became harder to make out in the growing gloom, she knew she must get back to the Ruin.

She hurried off the bridge and entered the trees.

Though the day was as calm as ever, a breath of air on her neck made her shiver. She tugged at her hood, but before she could pull it over her head, someone whispered in her ear. “Maeve, beware.”

It wasn’t the breeze. There was no breeze. And there was no mistaking the words. She spun around, but whoever had spoken to her had slid into the trees with the shadows.

Maeve started to run, and though she quickly put distance between herself and the bridge, she couldn’t outrun the words echoing in her head.

Maeve, beware.

She looked from tree to tree as she hurried toward the Ruin. Twice she thought she spied something moving, but it was only her imagination. She scolded herself for being silly. The forest would never turn against her.

Maeve slowed to a walk. Perhaps the voice had been warning her of something she hadn’t yet encountered—something that had nothing to do with the bridge or forest.

She didn’t want to think about that. It was bad enough imagining the worst of things she could see; if she started imagining the unknown, she would drive herself mad.

Her mind drifted back to the young woman she’d seen reflected in the stream. At first Maeve had thought she was looking at her own reflection. But the face belonged to someone else, and though the young woman hadn’t seemed threatening, there’d been an urgency about her.

She looked so much like Maeve. She had the same small mouth, green eyes, milk-white skin and the same thick mane of copper curls. Still, she was different—a little older and more solemn.

Who was she? Maeve had no answer—only questions. She was sure of one thing, though: the woman had appeared twice for a reason. The seer in Maeve must know something the blacksmith's daughter did not. *Maeve, beware.*

When Maeve arrived at the Ruin, the evening meal was beginning, so she slipped into her place, her mind awhirl with questions. She was halfway through her supper when a voice penetrated her thoughts.

"Well?"

Maeve looked up to see Bradan staring at her across the table. "Sorry," she replied, shaking her head to clear it. "What did you say?"

"I asked if you had learned why the Bridge of Whispers is so named."

Maeve stared past him toward the forest and once again found herself at the little bridge. "Yes," she replied, feeling breath on her neck and hearing the young woman whisper in her ear. "I think I have."

"I thought you would." To Maeve's surprise, he didn't press her for details. He simply nodded and returned to his supper.

It was not like Bradan to let her off that easily. He'd assigned her a task that took the entire day, yet now he didn't seem to care how she'd managed it. *Why?* Even so, she was relieved that he didn't press her for details. She couldn't explain the bridge's name without mentioning the young woman, and she wasn't prepared to do that. Odd as it was, she felt a closeness to her. And her instincts told her she must guard that.

Chapter 3

"How long do you expect to be away?" Maeve asked as she and Declan tramped across the field in front of the Ruin. The donkey in the distance was a black silhouette against the morning sun.

"Five or six days," he replied. "A week at most."

Maeve nodded. "I wish you weren't going."

Declan smiled. "I'll be home before you know it."

"I'm going to miss the little donkey."

"Are you saying you don't want me to go because I'm taking the donkey away? You're going to miss *him*, but not *me*?"

Maeve grinned and swatted Declan's arm. "Of course I shall miss you, but you're coming back. Traveller isn't."

Declan sniffed, feigning hurt feelings. Then he whistled, causing the donkey to look up from where he was grazing.

"Come on, Traveller," he beckoned him. "It's time to go."

The donkey seemed to consider the prospect but then went back to grazing.

Maeve laughed. "I think he's decided to stay.

Oh well." She shrugged. "It's lucky you're a bard and can tell a good story."

"Why is that?"

"The farmer will want to know why he isn't getting his donkey back."

Ignoring Maeve's jest, Declan called Traveller again, but this time the animal didn't even look up. "You *could* help me," he said. Then he shook his head. "Never mind. You wouldn't have any more luck than me. There's no reasoning with a donkey."

Maeve couldn't resist the dare. "We'll see about that," she said. "Come on, Traveller." She clapped her hands and chirruped. "That's a good fella."

The little donkey's ears twitched and he lifted his head. Then he brayed happily and trotted straight for her. Maeve turned to Declan and gloated, "What was so hard about that?"

"Show-off," he muttered as he slipped the halter over the donkey's head. "Come on, Traveller. It's time to live up to your name."

But the donkey was busy nuzzling Maeve's hand. She scratched his ears. "I'm sorry, Traveller. I have nothing for you this morning."

Undeterred, he began sniffing the pocket of her robe. She pushed his head away. "You clever little donkey. I can't fool you, can I?" She laughed and pulled a honey cake from her pocket. As the little donkey gobbled it up, she stroked his neck and murmured, "I shall miss you."

All the Druids had gathered at the front of the Ruin to see Finn and Declan off.

"Have a safe journey," Bradan said when the trio was ready to leave. The other Druids waved the bard and his apprentice on their way and then turned to get on with the day.

"Look." Maeve pointed to a young man running along the village road.

"Oh my," Enda said. "You'd think Dullahan, the headless horseman, was chasing him."

When he reached them, he skidded to a stop and doubled over, gasping for air. It took several attempts before he was able to speak.

"It is my wife!" he finally managed to say. "She's with child, and it is her time. She needs the birthing woman."

All eyes turned to Nora. She gestured to Enda. "Fetch my bundle. It's on the hook by my pallet." Then she turned to the young man. "Is this your wife's first child?"

He bobbed his head. "Yes, mistress."

Nora gave his arm a reassuring squeeze. "When did her pains begin?"

"Yesterday, it was. In the morning. Her mam came to help her, but naught has happened since then—except for the screaming. Even the village dogs cover their ears. But still there's no babe."

"First babies are often slow in coming," she assured him as Enda gave her the bundle of supplies. "I have my herbs. A cup of chamomile tea will work wonders. Come along. Take me to your wife."

It was late when Nora returned. She looked tired. Maeve put a pot of water on the boil for tea while Enda began to fix her mother some supper.

"Thank you, but no," Nora said wearily. "I have no stomach for food just now."

Enda's mouth tightened into a grim line. "Did it not go well?"

Nora shook her head. "Sadly, no. The babe was large and the wrong way around. Had I been called earlier, I might have been able to turn it, but things were too far along for that."

"The child died?"

"And the mother."

Maeve gasped, drawing the attention of both women.

"That is not the usual way of things," Nora assured her quickly. "In fact, until today I have never attended a birthing where both mother and babe were lost.

"Once, many years ago—Enda would've been about your age—I was called to the birthing of a baby where the mother died. She'd had a bad fall and the babe came early. The next day I attended another birth. It went well enough, except the cord wrapped itself around the babe. Poor thing never took a breath. Those two birthings—one coming on the heels of the other—made me doubt my calling. They haunted me for a long time. Eventually I pushed past them, but I've never forgotten." She paused and stared straight ahead, as if into another place and time. "I know I can't save all the babies, nor all the mothers, but that doesn't make it any easier."

Maeve was shocked and then saddened by the deaths of the woman and her child. It wasn't long, though, before the tragedy began gnawing at her in a different way. What if the same thing happened to Deirdre? According to Nora, mothers and babies did sometimes die, especially if a birthing woman wasn't there to assist.

Maeve kept telling herself Deirdre would be fine—she was young and healthy and strong. And yet ...

"For goodness' sake, girl," Bradan rebuked her sharply during one of their lessons. "Where is your mind? You haven't heard a word I've said this whole day."

Maeve's mind had been wandering—that was true enough. She shook her head. "I can't stop thinking about the birthing Nora went to."

The old man's expression softened. "Ah yes. I heard what happened. So now you're worried about your sister."

"It's getting near her time, and all I can think of is the young woman in the village."

Bradan nodded. “You know there are many more uneventful birthings than unfortunate ones, do you not?”

Maeve tapped her head. “My brain knows, but my heart isn’t convinced.”

He patted her hand. “You need to talk with Nora.”

So Maeve did.

When she told Nora her concerns, the older woman immediately pulled her into a hug. “What happened in the village is not the usual way of things. Mostly birthings are just hard work. But when it’s done and the mother is holding her child, she has already forgotten the discomfort. There’s no sense imagining the worst because it probably won’t happen.”

To Maeve’s relief, Nora not only calmed her worries, she told her what to expect and how to help Deirdre. That night, Maeve slept soundly, and when she awoke the next morning, she was more at peace than she had been for days.

“Good morning,” she waved and called across the meadow to Bradan, who was sitting in his usual spot among the oak trees. “What are we doing today?”

When she reached him, he gestured her to sit. “I’m glad to see you are anxious to get on with your lessons. We’re going to begin something new, and you’ll need to draw on all your senses.”

A hundred questions poured into Maeve’s mind, but she pressed her lips tightly together and held them in. No more blurting everything that came into her head. Bradan had said she needed to think more and speak less, and that was exactly what she was going to do. She would show him she *could* listen. She wasn't a child who needed constant reminding. In less than a week she would be fourteen—old enough to wed. Not that she had any plans to marry, but knowing she could if she chose to meant she was a woman, and she needed to start acting like one.

Maeve could tell Bradan was waiting for her to pounce on him with questions, and when she didn't, his expression turned to surprise. She almost laughed. It wasn't often she got the better of her teacher.

She offered him her brightest smile. "I'm ready."

Bradan cleared his throat. "In that case, let us begin. We have spent the last months studying dreams. They reflect a person's unguarded self and reveal things the conscious mind is unaware of. But there is more to being a seer than interpreting dreams. Today we shall begin our study of another divining tool."

He paused. Maeve knew he was waiting for her to press him for a clue, but she kept her mouth firmly shut.

He frowned. "Do you want to know what that tool is?"

She bobbed her head.

"Very well." He reached into the neck of his robe and drew a chain up over his head, holding it so that the translucent purple stone dangling from it spun and glinted in the morning sun.

"It's beautiful," Maeve said. She was mesmerized by the way the gem played with the light.

"It is an amethyst," Bradan told her. "But more importantly, it is a pendulum."

Once again a multitude of questions swarmed Maeve's mind, but she didn't give voice to a single one. She would wait for Bradan to tell her what he wanted her to know—even if it took every bit of willpower she possessed.

He laid the gemstone on his open palm and let the chain puddle around it. Though Maeve wanted to touch it, she clasped her hands in her lap.

Again Bradan paused as if waiting for her to say something, but when she didn't, he said, "This is much more than a pendant."

"You called it a pendulum."

"Yes." He nodded. "Do you know what a pendulum is? What it does?"

She shook her head. "No, but I'm sure you're going to tell me."

"Indeed." He lifted the necklace into the air once more. As it spun and swayed, he said, "A pendulum is a spiritual tool that helps us discover truths and make decisions."

How? The question sprang to Maeve's lips, but she held it in.

If Bradan noticed, he didn't let on. "The pendulum's power comes from the stone, which is a conduit for the energy of the person possessing it. If the connection between the pendulum and its owner is strong, the pendulum's power is mighty."

"So—" Maeve began but quickly bit back the rest of her question.

"What were you going to ask?" he prompted her.

"Nothing." She shook her head. "I shouldn't have interrupted. I'm sorry."

Bradan lowered the pendulum and squinted at Maeve.

She turned away.

"Look at me," he said. When she did, his expression softened. "Do you think I haven't noticed you biting your tongue?"

"I was trying to control my curiosity," she confessed. "You said I should speak less and think more. That's what I was trying to do."

"Your curiosity is a good thing, child," he replied. "It is one of your strengths."

"But you—" Maeve stopped when he raised a finger.

"It's how you deal with your curiosity that needs work. I want you to answer your own questions when you can. If thinking can provide the answers, that is what you should do. But that doesn't mean you must stop asking questions. When it is not possible for you to find the answer within yourself, of course you should ask me—or someone else. As in all things, it is a matter of balance."

"Balance again," she said. "I should have known."

Bradan chuckled. Then he returned the pendulum to his neck and allowed his fingers to trace the stone's shape through his robe. "This is my pendulum. It is my energy that flows through it. I will help you learn to harness your own, but before that can happen, you must find the right stone." He smiled. "As it happens, I think I know where that is."

Their trek through the forest was slow. Bradan was still weak from his recent illness, and Maeve didn't want to rush him. But it was a beautiful morning—more like spring than winter—and it was enough to be in the forest with her teacher.

Despite their leisurely pace, Bradan was weary by the time they arrived at the stream. Maeve spied a fallen log against a tree and led him to it. When he was settled, she shaded her eyes and looked skyward. The sun was nearly at its zenith, and a rumbling in her stomach said it was time to eat. She unwrapped the small bundle she'd brought and offered Bradan a sweet cake and a chunk of cheese.

For several minutes they ate in silence. Maeve turned her face to the sun, soaking up its warmth as if she were a newly sprouted seed poking through the earth. She turned to share this sensation with Bradan, but the look on his face kept her tongue still. He was staring at the Bridge of Whispers. Maeve followed his gaze, half expecting to see the red-haired woman. But she wasn't there. Or if she was, Maeve couldn't see her. Her gaze returned to Bradan. There was a sense of melancholy about him.

His expression cleared, and Maeve went back to her meal. Bradan had been having a private moment and she didn't want him to think she'd been spying.

He grinned and patted his stomach. "Thank you for bringing food. I can already feel my vigour returning."

"Good." Maeve smiled and then glanced toward the stream and its rocky banks. "This is where you think I'll find the stone for my pendulum?"

He laughed. "I am certain of it, though it won't be a simple task."

"No?" Maeve cocked her head.

He nodded toward the stream. "I believe your stone is in the brook, and the water will be cold."

Maeve shivered at the thought. There were probably thousands of rocks in the stream bed. *How was she supposed to find one particular stone?* She turned back to Bradan. "What exactly should I be looking for?"

"It is not your eyes that need to search out the stone, but your heart," he replied. "If you open your inner self, the stone will find *you*." He nodded to the stream once more. "It is time."

Maeve considered removing the cowhide boots laced around her legs but decided against it. Though they gave little protection from the cold, they would help her keep her footing. The rocks on the bank were slippery enough; those in the water would be even more treacherous.

"Find a walking stick," Bradan said, brandishing his own. "It will help you keep your feet."

Maeve nodded and looked around for a sturdy branch. Ready at last, she lifted her robe and mantle clear of the water, waded into the stream—and gasped as the shock of icy cold struck her. Even though Bradan had said her heart would find the stone, she peered into the stream.

From his place on the log, Bradan called instructions. "Concentrate on your task and you won't feel the cold. Open yourself wide. Let your heart reach out through your fingertips. Weigh the stones in your hand and discard the heavy ones."

After a time he became quiet, and when Maeve looked back he was dozing.

Clutching the stick and her clothing to her chest, she shut her eyes and opened her inner self. Then, steeling herself against the cold, she swept her free hand through the stream, allowing her fingers to slide over the larger rocks and seek out the pebbles clustered around them. One after the other she caressed them, inviting the perfect stone to find her. Moving on, she repeated the process over and over.

After searching with no luck for what felt like hours, she straightened and stretched. Her back was stiff from bending, and her hand and arm ached with cold. Her lower legs and feet had long ago grown numb. She looked back at Bradan. He was still asleep.

He was right. This was a challenging task. But if she hoped to find a stone for her pendulum before she froze to death, she'd best get on with it. She turned back to the water—and stopped. Standing in the stream directly in front of the Bridge of Whispers was the young woman with copper hair. She beckoned to Maeve.

Stepping carefully, Maeve pushed her way toward her through the icy stream. When the two were face to face, she stopped. The young woman smiled and looked into the water at her feet. Maeve followed her gaze but could detect nothing out of the ordinary. She saw rippling water—nothing more.

"I know you're trying to tell me something," she said to the young woman. "But I don't know what."

The young woman smiled again and then evaporated into the air.

"Don't go," Maeve stretched out her hand. But the young woman had disappeared—again.

Once more, Maeve looked into the stream. A single bubble rose up from the stream bed and broke the surface.

Cautiously Maeve started forward, her eyes focused on the place the bubble had appeared. Something was pulling her to the spot; it was the strangest sensation. She sensed she was exactly where she needed to be.

Reaching into the stream, she let the unknown force direct her hand and began raking through the stones on the bottom. No, no, no, no. Not this one. Not these either. And then her fingers closed around a stone smoother than the rest and lighter in weight. Despite the icy water, it pulsed with warmth in her hand. Maeve shut her eyes and smiled. She had found her pendulum.

Chapter 4

"Bradan! I found it!" Maeve cried as she worked her way to shore. "I found the stone for my pendulum!"

The old man blinked in confusion and squinted toward the stream.

With the stone clutched tight in her fist, she waved her hand in the air and grinned. "My pendulum. I found it!"

"Wonderful!" Bradan called back. "Be careful. You don't want to fall."

But in her excitement, Maeve forgot to tread carefully and down she went. Her walking stick cartwheeled in the air and landed with a splash an arm's length away.

"Oh, no!" she wailed as she assessed her situation. Though the stream was shallow, it came past her waist now that she was sitting in it. Her mantle and robe—both soaked—were floating just below the water's surface. Her nails were digging into her palm. She relaxed her grip but didn't open her hand. She could feel the small hard nub within. At least she hadn't lost the stone.

Bradan pulled himself to his feet. "Are you all right?"

Maeve attempted to stand, but the weight of her wet clothes kept pulling her down. "I'm fine," she called back when she finally found her footing, "except for being wetter than a kettle of washing." She stepped sideways and stretched to retrieve her walking stick. Drenched as she was, she needed it more than ever to drag herself out of the stream.

Finally she staggered to shore, and the water in her clothes rained onto the ground. As the puddle at her feet grew, Maeve began to feel lighter but far from comfortable. And far from warm. Her teeth were chattering. With her sopping skirt clinging to her legs, she picked her way along the rocky bank to Bradan.

"Oh my," he said. "We have to get you back to the Ruin before you catch your death of cold."

Maeve nodded. Despite the warm sunshine, she couldn't stop shivering.

"Take my cloak." Bradan fumbled with the clasp at his neck.

Maeve stayed his hand and shook her head. "You need it more than I do."

The old man looked dubious but didn't protest. "You must get back to the Ruin at once to change out of your wet things. Go on without me. I can make my own way back."

Maeve was uncertain. But she was also shivering uncontrollably. "Are you sure you'll be okay?"

Bradan scowled. "I'm not completely doddery. Just see me off these rocks and onto the path leading home."

Maeve took his arm. When they reached the safer footing of the forest, he said, "Now go."

She frowned. "Promise me you'll take your time. And stop to rest when you need to." Even when he nodded, she hesitated. Finally she pushed the stone into his hand and folded his fingers over it. "I'm afraid I'll drop it," she explained. And with a final squeeze of his hand, she started to run.

Enda's jaw dropped when Maeve burst into their sleeping quarters at the Ruin. "What happened?"

"I fell in the stream." Maeve started peeling off her wet things. "I'll be fine once I get into dry clothes. It's Bradan I'm concerned about."

Enda's eyes grew round. "He didn't fall in too, did he?"

"No, thank goodness, but he could see how cold I was and didn't want to slow me down, so he made me come back without him. He's returning on his own. But I'm afraid it will be too much for him."

Enda snatched her mantle from its hook. "Say no more. I shall find him and see him safely back. In the meantime—" She dug through her basket of herbs, pulled out a drawstring bag and tossed it to Maeve. "Make yourself some chamomile tea. It will take away the chill."

In dry clothes once more and wrapped in a fur rug, Maeve sat before the cooking fire, sipping a bowl of hot tea. Around her, the Druid women were preparing the evening meal.

"Let me help," Maeve offered but was glared into silence by Nora.

"If needs be, you'll sit by that fire until you turn to ash," the older woman declared. "You could have frozen to death, foolish girl. What on earth possessed you to wade into the stream in the middle of winter? And what was Bradan thinking to let you?" She shook her head and clucked her tongue. "You haven't a brain between you."

"Look!" Maeve threw off the rug and jumped up. "It's Enda and Bradan!" And before Nora could stop her, she raced across the meadow to meet them.

"How are you?" she said as she took Bradan's arm.

"I have a stone in my boot," he grumbled. "How it got there I have no idea, but it is most uncomfortable. More to the point, how are you?"

"Very warm." She fanned herself with her hand. "Nora has had me sitting in front of the fire for so long it's a wonder I haven't burst into flame." She nodded toward the long plank tables, where people were gathering. "But I'm fine. You, on the other hand, are very tired. I can see it in your eyes. You need a good supper and then your bed."

"That's what I told him too," Enda said.

"The tail has not yet started wagging the dog," Bradan retorted. "I'll decide what I—" But that's as far as he got. Enda and Maeve were both glowering at him, so he heaved a defeated sigh and closed his mouth.

The next morning Maeve arrived at the grove of oak trees long before her teacher. By the time Bradan showed himself, she'd worn a path in the grass from pacing. After her dunking in the stream, she'd forgotten about the stone, but now it was foremost in her thoughts.

"Do you have the crystal?" she blurted before Bradan had even sat down.

He scowled. "Good morning to you too."

The old Druid's glare hit the mark, and Maeve inwardly cringed. "Good morning," she mumbled and sat down opposite him.

Bradan looked up at the cloudless sky. "It's going to be a fine day," he announced, his features relaxing once more. "Considering our needs, it couldn't be better."

Maeve wondered what he meant.

He reached into the pocket of his robe and drew out a small bundle. Laying it on his lap, he pulled back the layers of cloth to reveal Maeve's stone.

She gasped. This was the first time she'd seen it. She'd held it of course, but she'd not seen it until this moment. It was beautiful—the size of her fingertip and shaped like a droplet of dew. She reached out, then pulled her hand back and looked to Bradan.

"May I touch it?"

"It is yours."

She laid the cloth on her lap, then hesitantly picked up the crystal and cupped it in her hand. Its warmth penetrated her palm and spread through her body. She lifted the stone skyward as if it were an offering and watched as it flashed in a rainbow of sparks.

"I've never seen anything like it," she murmured.

"It's clear quartz," he told her. "You are lucky it found you, for this stone makes the best sort of pendulum. Where exactly was it?"

Maeve lowered her arm and clasped the stone tightly in her hand. "By the Bridge of Whispers," she said, looking beyond Bradan as she went back in her mind and saw the red-haired woman gazing into the water. "She showed me."

"She?" Bradan's stiff tone jolted Maeve from her reverie.

She smiled nervously while her brain searched for an explanation that would erase her blunder. "Did I say *she*?"

Bradan regarded her suspiciously. "You did."

Maeve tried to stop smiling, but the idiotic grin seemed frozen to her face. "I guess I think of the stone as a girl." She shrugged and looked away. Bradan always seemed to know when she was hiding something. "Anyway," she hurried on before he could question her further, "the stone was near the arch of the bridge, and just as you said would happen, it found me. I saw a bubble rise from the bottom of the stream, and when I reached into the water, the stone practically jumped into my hand." She uncurled her fingers, stared down at the quartz and then at Bradan, her guilty smile finally gone. "I knew then it was the one."

Bradan looked as if he might say something, but his expression changed and he nodded. "That is the best way."

"So now do we turn it into my pendulum?" Maeve was anxious to steer the conversation onto safer ground.

"We shall make a start, but it will take some time before you have a working pendulum," said Bradan.

"Oh." Maeve was disappointed.

"First we must clear the quartz of the energy it has collected over time, so it is ready to accept your energy."

"How do we do that?"

"There are several ways. We could put it in a pouch with citrine, a crystal known for its cleansing qualities, but I have no such crystals. Another alternative is to expose it to the light of a full moon. But since the moon is far from full, we would have to wait several weeks."

Maeve felt her hopes flagging. "Is there anything we can do now?"

Bradan held out his hand for the stone. When Maeve passed it to him, he said, "There is. The sun can also clear energy from crystals—but one must take special care. While the moon works well for all crystals, the sun can damage some. Fortunately clear quartz can survive exposure to the sun." He gazed skyward once more. "And it's a gloriously sunny day."

Maeve's spirits again began to climb.

Bradan pulled himself to his feet with the aid of his walking stick. "I know just where to put the quartz for the sun to do its magic."

"Then I shall have my pendulum?" Maeve said hopefully.

Though Bradan's lips never moved, Maeve heard the old Druid's voice inside her head. "*Patience, child.*"

Aloud he said, "Then we must fill it with your energy."

Chapter 5

Since Bradan could teach Maeve nothing more until the sun had cleansed the crystal, her lessons came to a halt for the day. But the old man left her with a riddle. It was as old as time, he said, and simple to solve once you thought about it the right way. Maeve had no idea what the right way was, and after several hours of pondering, she was no closer to a solution than when Bradan had first posed the riddle.

What creature walks on four legs in the morning, two legs at noon, and three in the evening?

Like dreams, riddles relied on symbols for their meaning. Unfortunately, knowing that didn't help Maeve determine what the legs were symbols for or what morning, noon and evening represented. As she puzzled over the conundrum, time stood still.

The sun hadn't moved in hours. The day—and this riddle—were going to last forever.

When darkness finally chased the sun into hiding and Maeve prepared for bed, she was still baffled. But as she burrowed beneath her blanket, she banished the riddle from her mind.

Her thoughts immediately returned to the quartz crystal and the pendulum it would become. She hadn't the slightest notion how pendulums worked or why they were useful, but as she waited for sleep to still her mind, her head danced with possibilities.

The night passed as slowly as the day had, and after hours of tossing and turning, Maeve was certain she was going to go mad if she lay in bed a second longer. Though the sky was still black as tar, she stole from her pallet and felt her way to the stone bench in front of the Ruin. She stared hard at the eastern sky, willing the sun to rise. But the morning refused to show itself before its time.

When it did finally arrive, Maeve was the only one who noticed. The Druids took longer than usual to rise, and even then they moved in slow motion. Everything about the morning was sluggish. The fire was slow to catch, the porridge was reluctant to bubble and the water for washing-up remained icy cold long after it should have boiled. And for the second day in a row, Bradan was tardy joining Maeve in the copse of oak trees.

"I apologize for making you wait," he said when he at last appeared and took his seat. He reached into the pocket of his robe. "I was preparing your pendulum." With a flourish he extended his arm, and a silver chain swooped from his fingers. At the end of it spun Maeve's crystal, encased in a tight web of slender silver wire suspended from a finely wrought chain.

She regarded her teacher with amazement. "You did this?"

He shrugged, then slipped the pendulum over Maeve's head. The chain was cool against her skin, but the quartz was warm. She held it to her chest and closed her eyes, feeling the comfort of it flow through her body.

"Yes, yes. That's right," Bradan said, but his voice was far away and muffled as though he were speaking through water.

Maeve opened her eyes to see him smiling and nodding.

"It feels magical," she said.

He nodded. "It is a portal to your soul."

She closed her eyes again and smiled. "My pendulum."

"Soon," Bradan said.

Maeve's eyes flew open and she clutched the quartz as if she expected him to snatch it back. "Are you saying it is still not ready? I thought it just needed the sun to purify it."

"That was the first step. Now you must charge it with your own energy."

"How do I do that?"

"You are doing it now. The bond between you and the quartz was strong before the sun did its work. All you need do is keep the stone close to you, open your spirit and allow the energy to flow from you to it."

"How long will that take?"

"Usually several days—even a week, though

I suspect your crystal will charge more quickly. I wouldn't be surprised if it is ready tomorrow."

Maeve pressed the crystal to her breast. Its warmth pulsed in rhythm with her heart. "Then what?"

"Then I will teach you the way of it."

Maeve grinned and hugged herself.

"If"—the old man regarded her sternly—"you can tell me the answer to the riddle I posed yesterday."

Maeve felt as if he had dumped icy water over her head. If mastering her pendulum hinged on solving the riddle, she might as well throw the crystal back into the stream.

Maeve walked along the tables in front of the Ruin, laying down bowls and spoons for the midday meal. Behind her the women were readying the food, while the men—summoned by the hearty aroma of mutton stew—made their way to the benches.

Maeve was concentrating on Bradan's riddle, and it wasn't until everyone began shouting and hurrying toward the edge of the woods that she was pulled from her thoughts.

She looked to see what had set off the exodus, but her view was blocked by mantles flying and arms waving.

Dropping the bowls and spoons, she lifted her skirt and started running too. When she heard someone call "Finn!" she began to run with real purpose. Declan was back.

She watched Declan's mother swallow him up in a ferocious hug while his little sister latched onto his leg. His father showed more restraint, merely squeezing his shoulder and grinning, the edges of his mouth practically touching his ears. *Like father, like son*, Maeve thought, for the grin on Declan's face was every bit as big.

She drank him in with her eyes. She couldn't get enough of him—his laughing eyes and teasing smile, the dimple that creased one cheek when he smiled, and the way a lock of hair slid down his forehead and into his eyes no matter how many times he pushed it back.

As if reading her thoughts, Declan swept back the wayward curl, then looked up at her and winked. Maeve felt the colour rise in her cheeks. Through her robe the quartz crystal pulsed in time with her hammering heart. She took a deep breath to clear her head. How was it the mere sight of Declan could fluster her so?

Maeve sloshed a stick about in a cauldron of scalding wash water and gazed longingly toward the edge of the forest where Declan was chopping firewood. When Finn freed him from his lessons, the two had hoped to spend the afternoon together, but, as usual, chores came first.

Cara lumbered toward Maeve beneath an

armful of dirty laundry. She clucked her tongue. "You're not stirring honey into your tea, my girl. Put your back into the work."

"Yes, Cara," Maeve mumbled and bore down on the stick. She'd no sooner put more weight behind her efforts than there was a sharp crack and the stick snapped. The next thing Maeve knew, she was somersaulting through the air. Narrowly missing the cauldron of hot water, she landed with a thud onto the grass. She sat up and blinked at the splintered end of the stick still in her hand.

Cara dropped the laundry and hurried to her. "Are you hurt?"

Maeve shook her head and, accepting Cara's outstretched hand, pulled herself to her feet. "Surprised is all. This stick is done for though." She tossed it into the fire. "I'd best find another."

Before she'd started for the woods, a familiar voice called to her from the entrance of the Ruin.

"Maeve." Enda waved and hurried toward her. "I need you to do something for me."

Maeve gestured to the laundry tub. "I'm helping Cara with the washing."

"Never mind that," Enda said. "I'll help Cara. I've been stuck inside all day. I could use some fresh air and human company. But I'm almost out of coltsfoot—I need it to treat Bradan's cough. The plants grow by the pond at the other end of the meadow. They're easy to find—miniature suns with pink stems."

Maeve was pleased to be freed from laundry duties, but she didn't let on. She pointed to the woodland. "First I need to fetch a stick to stir the wash."

Enda's eyes crinkled mischievously. "You might want to ask Declan to accompany you. Your basket could get heavy."

As Enda had predicted, the brilliant yellow coltsfoot flowers were sprinkled liberally throughout the meadow surrounding the pond, and Maeve's basket was soon overflowing. Still, the young people lingered.

Declan scanned the grass. "I think we've picked every coltsfoot flower there is." Then, reaching for the basket, he added, "We should start back."

Maeve fell in step beside him. "It feels like we just got here. You haven't even told me about your journey."

"What would you like to know?"

"Was Traveller pleased to be home?"

Declan rolled his eyes. "Of course the donkey is the first thing you want to know about."

"Well, he *was* the reason for the journey."

"True enough," he conceded, "To be honest, he looked unhappy to see us leave."

"Really? Or was it *you* who was unhappy to leave *him*?" she teased.

Declan shrugged. "As far as donkeys go, he is likable enough."

Maeve grinned. "Yes, he is. And I miss him."

"So you keep saying. Why are you so attached to him? He's just a donkey."

Maeve detected an irritated tone in Declan's voice, and for a moment she regarded him curiously. Then she laughed. "You're jealous."

He glowered at her. "Don't be ridiculous. Why would I be jealous of a donkey?"

"Because he's a handsome fellow and I'm fond of him."

Declan's jaw dropped. "You think he's *handsome*?" He shook his head and stomped off toward the Ruin.

You are jealous, Maeve thought and then called after him, "I think you're handsome too."

Declan stopped in mid-stride and spun around. "Are you comparing me to a donkey now?"

More laughter bubbled up inside Maeve, but she held it in and ran after him. "No," she said when she'd caught up. "Of course not. It's you who's doing that."

Declan didn't reply. But he didn't stalk off again either, so Maeve continued. "I'm flattered that you're jealous."

"I am not jealous," he snapped.

Maeve slid her arm through his. "Well, you needn't be. You are the most important person in my life. Don't you know that?"

Declan stopped walking and turned to face her. "I'm sorry. I know I'm being foolish. It's just that we have so little time together I don't want to share you any more than I have to—especially with a donkey."

A lump lodged itself in Maeve's throat.

"I know we said we would be friends for now," Declan continued. "We are both busy with our lessons. There is barely time for eating and sleeping."

Maeve nodded.

"The thing is," he rushed on, "you are already more than a friend. I feel you with me wherever I go—whatever I do. You're my soul shadow."

"I like that." Maeve smiled shyly. Her heart was so full she feared it would burst.

Declan took her hand and they resumed walking. After a time Maeve said, "What else did you do on your journey? Did Finn teach you more stories?"

"He did," Declan nodded. "And I was happy for it. It helped pass the miles of an uneventful journey." He paused. "Well, mostly uneventful. There was one thing."

Maeve's curiosity was piqued. "What was that?"

"After we returned the donkey, we stopped at a nearby farm so Finn might visit with a friend."

"And?" Maeve said.

"The fellow had news about Queen Ailsa and King Owen. King Redmond has spared them."

Really?" Maeve said, "Did he let them go free?"

Declan shook his head. "No. He wasn't that forgiving. He imprisoned them. Well, King Owen anyway. He's in chains in the dungeon of the Great King's castle."

"What of Queen Ailsa?" Maeve asked.

"King Redmond was much more lenient with her. Despite betraying him, she is his wife. So he exiled her to a small castle not far from his own. She is guarded but free to move about—even into the gardens."

"Do you think that is wise?"

Declan shrugged. "The Great King is a merciful man. Now it's your turn. What has happened with you while I've been gone?"

Maeve told him about falling into the stream as she tried to find a stone for her pendulum. Then she showed him the quartz crystal.

"It's beautiful," he said.

"Bradan thinks that perhaps by tomorrow it will be charged with my energy and I can finally begin learning to use it." She frowned. "That is if I can give him the answer to a riddle he posed yesterday." The word puzzle was burned into Maeve's brain, and she recited it without conscious thought. "What creature walks on four legs in the morning, two legs at noon, and three in the evening?"

"Hmmn," Declan murmured. "I've not heard that one before."

They had nearly reached the Ruin, and Maeve shaded her eyes against the sun to see what was happening. The washtub had been put away and the bushes were draped with wet wash. It would soon be time to begin the evening meal, but for the time being the day's work was done, and Maeve felt herself relax.

She spied Enda on the road, speaking to a woman with a small child. The tot was squirming in the woman's arms so she put him on the ground. He immediately got on all fours and began crawling toward the trees, forcing his mother to chase after him.

Maeve turned her attention back to the Ruin, where Bradan was sitting on the stone bench. She smiled and waved. He waved back, pulled himself up and, leaning heavily on his walking stick, moved to meet her.

Maeve abruptly stopped as the singsong words of the riddle that had been playing in the back of her mind came to the fore.

What creature walks on four legs in the morning, two legs at noon, and three in the evening?

To her immense surprise and relief, there was the answer—as obvious as the sun breaking free of a bank of clouds. Maeve's spirits soared. Tomorrow she would learn the secrets of her pendulum.

Chapter 6

The next morning when Bradan asked Maeve the riddle, she blurted the answer.

"A person."

The old Druid raised an eyebrow. "Are you certain?"

"Yes," she said, though her teacher's gaze was making her doubt herself. "It was just as you said. Once I thought about it the right way, it was simple to solve."

The intensity left the old Druid's eyes and the hard line of his mouth softened. Maeve felt the tension drain from her.

"You are correct. In the morning of our lives we crawl on all fours, walk on two legs as adults and with the aid of a stick when we are old. Well done. Did it take you long to glean the meaning?"

Maeve opened her mouth to reply but then closed it again.

"Why do you hesitate?"

"I'm not sure. I thought about the riddle for a very long time," she said, "but when the answer finally came to me, I wasn't thinking about it at all."

Bradan's face broke into a wide grin. "Perfect!"

Maeve pulled back in surprise. "What is?"

He chuckled. "I have been telling you to trust your mind and heart to lead you to the truth. Examine the questions, yes, but then step back and allow your inner mind to weigh the facts against your instincts. Only then will you find the true meaning of things. And that is precisely what you've done. Now that you know how to find that balance, you can move forward with your lessons more confidently." He patted her hand. "And that means you are ready to master your pendulum."

Maeve's heart began to race, and her hand moved to the stone at her neck. Even through the cloth, she could feel its warmth filling her with calm and opening her mind.

Bradan began to speak. "You have shared your energy with your pendulum, so now it is an extension of your mind and spirit. It knows everything you know and everything you suspect you know—even things you have no idea you know."

"What sorts of things?"

"Knowledge carried over from your time in the Otherworld. Also experiences you had as a babe but have forgotten. There is much hidden within you. While the mind can become muddled and your spirit congested with a plethora of emotions, your pendulum always finds a clear path.

"To be a seer is to be in touch with your higher self, the part of you that remembers, interprets and understands all that you are and do, including your past and your future. Our higher selves encompass much more than our immediate being." He lifted his pendulum from around his neck and dangled it in the air. "Your pendulum will help you do that."

Maeve nodded. During her life there had been times when she'd known things she couldn't possibly know. At other times she'd been maddeningly frustrated as she searched for memories and nuggets of knowledge she was certain she possessed but which refused to show themselves.

Maeve started to remove her pendulum, but Bradan stilled her hand. "First let me show you. A pendulum is a personal talisman and will work only for the person to whom it belongs. My pendulum knows my truths, but it can tell me nothing about you unless that knowledge is somehow related to me. Watch closely."

The old man gripped his stick and stood, planting his feet firmly on the ground. He rolled his shoulders and stretched one arm away from his body. Holding the chain loosely between his thumb and index finger, he let the amethyst dangle until it ceased spinning. Once it was still, he closed his eyes and murmured something Maeve didn't catch. When he opened his eyes again he said, "May I ask you some questions?"

The amethyst began swaying gently from side to side. How had Bradan done that? She'd focused on him the whole time, and he hadn't moved a muscle.

"Thank you." When the gem stopped moving he said, "Is my name Bradan?"

The amethyst swayed from side to side once more.

"Thank you," Bradan said again, and again the pendulum came to a stop. "Am I an old man?" Once more the pendulum swayed back and forth. As before, he thanked it and asked, "Will I live forever?" This time, instead of swaying from side to side, the amethyst carved a circle in the air. The Druid thanked the pendulum a final time, lowered his arm and sat down.

"Well?" he asked. "What did you observe?"

"Well," she began, "you spoke to the pendulum as though it were a person. You were courteous and respectful."

She glanced at Bradan for confirmation, and when he nodded, she continued. "You murmured something before you started, and you asked the pendulum for permission to speak with it."

Again Bradan nodded. "I offered a blessing to nature in thanks, and I asked for the pendulum's consent because it isn't always in a mood to respond."

Maeve was surprised. "Pendulums have moods?"

"Indeed. Some days they are unwilling to engage in a conversation, so to save a body grief, it is best to inquire in advance. If my pendulum remains still when I ask permission, I know it won't cooperate. What did you notice about the questions themselves and the way the pendulum responded?"

Maeve frowned. "You asked questions you already knew the answers to."

"That is true."

"Why? What point is there if you already know the answer?"

"You tell me."

Of course Bradan wouldn't simply answer her question. She thought for a moment. "I suppose it was so you would know if your pendulum was telling the truth."

"That is so," the old man replied. "And to determine the motion the pendulum would use to answer. Before I pose questions I don't know the answers to, I must be sure I understand how the pendulum will communicate with me."

"Is it not always the same?" Again Maeve was surprised.

He shook his head. "Pendulums can be as fickle as people. Did you notice anything else about the questions?"

Maeve replied without hesitation. "They could all be answered with a yes or a no. Side to side for yes and in a circle for no."

He smiled. "Good. You have done well. Now it is time for you to learn the ways of your own pendulum."

Maeve's heart skipped a beat and her hands shook as she removed her pendulum. It was finally time. She felt as if she was about to pass through a hidden portal and discover something of herself as yet unknown. She had felt a oneness with the crystal from the moment her fingers had first touched it in the stream. It was a piece of her that had been missing her whole life but was now found.

If Bradan sensed her heightened anticipation, he didn't let on. "The way you hold the pendulum is very important. Do as I do."

They both stood and Bradan stretched out his arm. Then he let his pendulum dangle until it became still. Maeve did the same.

"Good," he said. "It is very important that the pendulum comes to rest completely between questions."

Maeve nodded.

"Let us begin. Offer a blessing to nature in thanks for your gift and this opportunity to speak with your pendulum."

Maeve shut her eyes and said, "With a full heart I thank the forest, especially the stream, for sharing this crystal and all its wisdom with me. I promise to use it well." To her ears the blessing sounded inadequate. She looked to her teacher for guidance. Smiling encouragement, he gestured for her to continue.

Maeve looked down at the pendulum dangling from her fingers. It was swaying slightly, so she concentrated on calming her shaking arm until the crystal became still. "May I ask you some questions?" she said. Would her pendulum respond?

After a few very long seconds the crystal began to move—but not from side to side as Bradan's amethyst had done. Maeve's crystal began carving an arc in the air. No! Horrified, she looked to her teacher.

"There is no need to be alarmed," he said. "Remember this is your pendulum—not mine. It may respond differently. Ask a question for which the answer is yes. If the pendulum moves in the same way, you will know a circular motion is a positive reply."

Maeve took a deep breath to calm herself, and when the pendulum was perfectly still she closed her eyes and asked, "Is my name Maeve?" Afraid of what the answer might be, she kept her eyes squeezed shut, but when she felt the pendulum move, she had to look. Once more it was tracing a circle in the air. For a brief second she panicked. And then she remembered that a circular motion was a negative response for Bradan's pendulum. For hers it must mean yes. She let out a relieved sigh and thanked her pendulum.

"Now ask a question for which the answer is no," the old man told her.

Maeve waited for the pendulum to stop moving and then said, "Is Bradan my father?"

Once again the pendulum moved in a circle, and once more Maeve turned with worry to her teacher. "It's not working! You aren't my father, but the pendulum says you are!"

Bradan regarded her sternly. "You must be

more observant. What direction was the pendulum turning?"

Maeve drew a circle in the air with her finger.

Bradan nodded. "Now ask a question for which the response should be yes."

When the pendulum became still, she asked again, "Is my name Maeve?" When the pendulum began circling, she noted it was doing so in the opposite direction. She was immediately relieved. "Thank you, pendulum. Oh, thank you."

"Now," Bradan said, "you want to ask a question for which the outcome is still to be determined. It could go either way and therefore the pendulum can't answer with certainty."

Maeve regarded Bradan curiously. "What help is that?"

"It lets you know the pendulum's response for 'perhaps,' and it tells you that when it responds that way, your actions will decide the matter."

Maeve nodded and searched her mind for a question. Finally she said, "Pendulum, will I ever master my thoughts?" She immediately regretted her choice. What if it answered no?

When the crystal began to sway from side to side, she turned to Bradan. "Perhaps?"

He nodded. "It's up to you to make it a yes."

For the rest of the morning Bradan showed Maeve the ways of her pendulum, and she absorbed his teachings as never before. Her mind soaked up her teacher's words as effortlessly as her lungs took in air. She couldn't get enough of this new divining tool. When the sun reached its zenith and the old Druid declared it was time for her to practice alone, Maeve was ready.

It was the chance she'd been waiting for. She had so many things to ask her pendulum. Things she didn't want to share with Bradan—or anyone. She couldn't even wait for the midday meal. As soon as Bradan released her, she stuffed cheese, bread and some dried berries into her pocket and set off.

She needed to go somewhere she wouldn't be interrupted, and she knew just the place: the Bridge of Whispers. It was where she'd found the quartz, so she hoped her pendulum would be at ease there and more willing to answer her questions. Bradan said pendulums could be moody, and Maeve wanted to put hers in the best mood possible.

She ran the whole way to the stream, welcoming the rush of wind through her hair. She held tight to the pendulum around her neck. She couldn't risk losing it. The closer she got to the stream, the warmer the stone grew beneath her fingers. She smiled. It knew where they were going.

She didn't stop until she was standing in the centre of the bridge. As she waited for her ragged breathing to slow, she took the crystal from her neck, cupped it in her hand and watched it play with the sunlight. Then when her breathing became steady once more, she held out her arm and allowed the pendulum to dangle from her fingers. She uttered a blessing and worked through the steps Bradan had taught her.

When she was ready to move from questions about things she knew to the things she wanted to know, Maeve glanced about to be sure she was alone and focused on slowing her racing heart.

One question had been plaguing her for weeks. Though she was afraid to hope the pendulum might know the answer, she had to ask. Her words came out in a rush. "Pendulum, am I imagining the young woman I keep seeing at the Bridge of Whispers?" She stared hard at the quartz crystal, willing it to carve a no circle in the air, but holding her body still as a statue so she didn't move the pendulum herself.

For what seemed like forever, the crystal remained still—as if it hadn't heard. Maeve was about to ask her question again when she felt the chain shift in her fingers. As she watched the quartz on the end of the silver chain, she held her breath.

It started to move—in a small circle at first, but then the arcs became larger, pushing forcefully through the air. Was that yes or no? Maeve was so rattled she couldn't remember which direction was which. Think! In her mind she pictured the pendulum's response to her question, "Is my name Maeve?" The answering circle had definitely rotated the other way.

She hadn't imagined the young woman. She was real!

Maeve thanked the pendulum and dropped her arm. She couldn't stop trembling. She spun around to scan the stream and its banks, half expecting to see the young woman—hoping she would see her.

Maeve cradled the pendulum to her cheek. It was warm. "Thank you. Oh, thank you," she whispered, meaning the words with all her heart. She needed the young woman to be real. She didn't know why it was so important—only that it was.

Now that she was certain the woman existed, Maeve had many more questions. Who was she? What was her name? Why did she keep appearing? What did her warning mean? But none of those questions could be answered with a yes or no. Maeve would have to ask another way, but she couldn't think what that might be.

Even so, she wasn't ready to put her pendulum away. Bradan was forever chastising her for her endless questions. Now that she had the chance to ask as many as she wanted, she wasn't about to squander it. She might not be able to learn anything more about the red-haired girl, but there were other things she could ask. One thing had been niggling at her ever since Bradan had told her she had the gift of sight.

She stretched out her arm and waited for the pendulum to become still.

"Pendulum," she said, "am I a Druid?"

She stared at the crystal, steeling herself for the no she knew would come.

As the pendulum began to circle, Maeve's eyes grew wide. Yes? She thanked the pendulum, waited for it to stop moving and asked another question for which she knew the answer was yes. The pendulum responded accordingly. Maeve repeated her original question. "Am I a Druid?" The pendulum's answer was the same.

Maeve didn't know what to think. Bradan had assured her the pendulum wouldn't lie, but how could this be true? Her parents weren't Druids so how could she be one? Unless—

Maeve steadied her arm. "Pendulum, is Eamon the blacksmith my father?" As the pendulum began to rotate in a no direction, Maeve gasped. She thanked the pendulum and it became still once more. "Is Bronagh my mother?" Again the pendulum told her no.

A floodgate of emotions opened inside Maeve, sweeping her life away as if it had never existed. No wonder her parents had never cared for her. They weren't her parents. The life she'd lived with them hadn't been a happy one, but it had still defined her existence. And even though she'd felt like a misfit, she'd had a place. Now that was gone and she was floating in an abyss. She had no past and no kin—nothing to ground her, nothing to hang on to. She felt more lost than ever.

An image of Deirdre flashed into her mind. Did this mean Deirdre was lost to Maeve as well?

Fanning a spark of hope, Maeve once more turned to her pendulum. "Is Deirdre my sister?"

The pendulum responded without hesitation, and Maeve's arm dropped listlessly to her side.

Returning the crystal to its place around her neck, Maeve started back to the Ruin. Though her mind was racing, the rest of her felt dead.

She was a Druid. It's what Maeve had hoped for. But the knowledge brought her no joy. She may have been born a Druid, but she'd been raised as a blacksmith's daughter. She didn't belong to either of those worlds. She hadn't discovered who she was—only who she wasn't.

Why hadn't she been raised a Druid? Who were her real parents? Why wasn't she with them? How had she ended up with the blacksmith and his wife? Why hadn't they told her the truth?

And then there was the matter of the copper-haired woman she kept seeing at the Bridge of Whispers. Maeve wanted to know who she was and why she kept seeing her. The young woman's ability to come and go at will must mean she was a spirit, but what sort? Was she to be trusted or feared? She seemed friendly. She'd helped Maeve find the crystal and she'd warned her of danger, though she hadn't said what that danger was.

So many questions—and no answers. Perhaps it was time to consult Bradan. He wanted her to work things out for herself when she could, but she didn't see how that was possible this time. The things she needed to know she couldn't figure out by thinking, and her pendulum could only tell her yes or no.

Then she had an unsettling thought. What if Bradan didn't know the answers either?

"You're off to the village again tomorrow?" Nora looked askance at her daughter as they prepared for bed that night. "Weren't you just there?"

"There are twin boys with coughs," Enda explained. "I need to see if the herbs I left have done their job, and I want to give their mother a salve for their chests."

Nora nodded.

"Do you need anything while I'm there?"

"I'll think on it and let you know in the morning," her mother replied.

Enda turned to Maeve. "What about you?"

Startled from her thoughts, Maeve forced herself back into the moment. "I'm sorry. What did you say?"

Enda chuckled. "I asked if you needed anything from the village. I'm going tomorrow. You could come with me if you like."

"I can't miss my lessons right now. Bradan is teaching me to use my pendulum." Her hand went to the stone at her neck.

"We'll go some other time," Enda said. "I would happily visit the village every day. So much hustle and bustle and so many people to talk to. Just yesterday I met a woman from the Midlands. Very friendly she was—interested in everything. We chatted ever so long. She asked about ..."

Though Maeve nodded and smiled, she was barely listening. She was too busy trying to make sense of the tangle of questions in her head.

Chapter 7

By the time Maeve made her way to the copse of oak trees the next morning, she had convinced herself the things her pendulum had told her could not be true. She'd been so anxious to have her questions answered that she must have influenced the movement of the crystal without realizing. Bradan said that sometimes happened. And since she didn't want him to think she was incapable of mastering her pendulum, she decided to say nothing.

"Good morning," Bradan said. "How did you get on with your pendulum yesterday?"

Maeve flopped down onto the stump. "I think I'm doing something wrong." So much for her resolve to say nothing.

Bradan cocked his head. "Did your pendulum not respond?"

She shrugged. "Yes, but I know the answers can't be right."

"Why do you say that?"

Maeve looked away. "You'll think I'm foolish."

"I very much doubt that," he assured her. "You couldn't have asked your pendulum anything more outrageous than the questions I've put to mine. I once inquired if there was a way of stretching my tongue so I could touch my nose with it." He chortled and slapped his knee.

Maeve regarded him with amused surprise. "You really asked that?"

He nodded. "I did. Of course the answer was no, but it was weeks before I stopped trying. What was your question?"

Maeve's smile faded. "Last year when you told me I had the gift of sight, I didn't believe you. Only Druids are seers. Then after I interpreted the Great King's dream, I began to think you might be right. Perhaps I was a seer. But—" She stopped.

"You asked your pendulum if you are a Druid."

She nodded.

"And it said you were."

"Yes." She searched Bradan's face for an explanation. "Why would it tell me that?"

The old man looked directly into her eyes. "Because you are."

Maeve scowled and clucked her tongue. "Living among Druids and learning Druid ways doesn't make me one."

"No, it doesn't," he agreed.

"Then why—"

He lifted a hand to quiet her. "There is something I have been meaning to tell you for some time, but I've been waiting for the right moment. It would seem that moment is now."

Maeve inched forward on the stump.

"You are not my only apprentice," he began. "Years ago there was another young woman such as yourself. And like you, she was amazingly gifted." A flurry of questions popped into Maeve's mind, but she bit them all back.

"Her name was Ciara." The old man paused. "She was your mother."

A door slammed shut inside Maeve's mind. Even though Bradan was confirming what her pendulum had told her, she would not allow herself to believe him. "No. That isn't possible. Eamon and Bronagh are my parents."

Bradan's gaze remained steady. "Not your birth parents."

Her life as the blacksmith's daughter had been horrid, but it was all she had to hang on to. "They have to be," Maeve insisted. "Why would they keep me if I wasn't their child? They couldn't abide me." Her eyes narrowed. "You're making this up."

Bradan looked skyward for a moment and then back at Maeve. "My words shatter the world as you know it. I understand. But it doesn't change the truth. If you won't accept my word on the matter, perhaps Nora can convince you."

Maeve pulled back. "Nora! What does she have to do with this?"

Bradan dragged himself to his feet. "She attended your birth. Ask her what happened. If you tell her I sent you, she will speak freely. When you are satisfied that I am being truthful with you, we shall talk again." Then, leaning heavily on his stick, he made his way back to the Ruin.

Maeve found Nora in front of the Ruin with the rest of the women preparing sheep's wool for spinning. Some were separating wads of shorter hairs from the longer ones, while others stood over steaming vats of soapy water, washing away the dirt and grease.

"No lessons this morning?" Nora asked as she lumbered, bearing a basket of wet wool, toward a table.

Maeve followed behind. "I do, but Bradan has sent me to"—she paused and lowered her voice—"uncover truths."

"About cleaning wool?" Nora chuckled as she dropped the basket onto the table and set about separating the clumps. She beckoned Maeve to help her.

"No," Maeve said, reaching into the basket. "About Ciara's child."

"What do you know of Ciara?"

The bottom dropped out of Maeve's stomach. So Ciara was real. "Only that she was my mother," Maeve mumbled.

Nora fell back a step and squinted at Maeve as if seeing her for the first time. "Of course," she said at last. "Why didn't I see it?" She reached out and touched Maeve's hair. "You are so like her."

It was true then. Ciara was her mother. Maeve didn't know what to think.

"Bradan said you would tell me what happened when I was born."

"To be truthful, I know very little—and Bradan swore me to secrecy about even that."

"If you'd rather not speak of it, I understand." Nora had already confirmed that Ciara was her mother. Maeve would get the rest of the story from Bradan.

Nora patted her hand. "No, no. I can see the truth of things just by looking at you." And without further hesitation, she launched into her story.

"Ciara was with child and quite near her time when she went into hiding."

Maeve frowned. "Why was she hiding?"

"I don't know. No one did," Nora said and then added, "except Bradan of course.

"About a week after Ciara left the Ruin, one of the lads came to me in a panic. He said Bradan had sent him to fetch me. I was to go immediately and say nothing to anyone. So I snatched up my kit and hurried after the boy into the woods.

"We found Bradan on a narrow trail hidden by ferns. He was kneeling beside Ciara. She was bleeding from a head wound. I could see she was in a bad way."

"What had happened to her?"

"Bradan didn't say and I knew better than to ask. But there was a bloody rock on the ground beside her."

"Were you able to get her back to the Ruin?"

Nora shook her head. "There wasn't time. It was clear she was dying, but she was also in labour. And she was determined to see you born." She lowered her eyes. "Your mother lived long enough to hold you and make Bradan swear to keep you safe."

Maeve's heart twisted in her chest. So this was what it felt like to be loved. She was both crushed and elated. If only her mother hadn't died. A tear slid down her cheek. She brushed it away. "Then what happened?"

"Bradan feared your life was in danger. We couldn't take you to the Ruin. So he took you to a nearby cave and I fetched a wet nurse to care for you until arrangements could be made.

"An opportunity presented itself the very next day. A woman from another village had come to be with her sister during her confinement. But the journey brought on her pains, and I was called to attend her at a farm just outside the village. Bradan thought it might be an opportunity to find a safe home for you—perhaps the woman could be convinced she'd given birth to twins. So he came along and hid with you in the bushes.

"The woman fainted as soon as she gave birth. The child was stillborn. But I pretended all was well and sent the woman's sister on an errand so that Bradan and I might exchange you for the dead child. When the woman awoke, she was none the wiser and you were safe."

Nora shrugged. "And that's all I know. I never asked who the woman was nor where she hailed from. It was meant to be a secret, and until now it has been. No one at the Ruin ever speaks of that time. Only Bradan knows the whole story."

Maeve made her way back to the copse of oak trees after the midday meal. Her conversation with Nora left no room for doubt. She was a Druid. Instead of settling matters, however, the certainty only confused and aggravated Maeve more. Why had Bradan kept it a secret from her? The longer she waited for the old man, the more she paced and fumed.

"I am so angry," she sputtered when he finally arrived. "You swore you would never deceive me again. And yet you've known all along who my mother was, but you've kept that from me. Don't you think I have a right to know?"

"Sit," he said, ignoring Maeve's outburst and gesturing to her usual perch.

Her mouth dropped open. How dare he act as if she were a child throwing a tantrum! She jammed her hands onto her hips. "I don't want to sit. What I want is for you to answer me."

Once more he gestured to the tree stump. "That's precisely what I intend to do. But you might as well be comfortable."

Maeve scowled. Part of her clung to her indignation, but another part wanted the truth, so she sat.

Bradan nodded. "Good." And then he began.

"Ciara's parents—your grandparents—were both seers, so your mother came by her gift naturally. Even when she was young it was clear to all that her abilities were exceptional. Unlike you, Ciara had known of her gift her whole life, and by the time she was sixteen, her skills were already being sought by royalty."

A cloud seemed to pass over Bradan. Maeve could tell the memory of Ciara troubled him deeply.

But he continued his story. "The girl walked in sunshine, spreading warmth and light wherever she went. She was much loved by the people." He paused. "By most people—though not all. There were those who mistrusted her goodness—for it was a condition they had never known—and so it was they sought to destroy her."

"Nora said she went into hiding," Maeve interrupted. "Was that why?"

Bradan nodded.

Maeve hesitated before asking her next question. "Nora also said a bloody rock was found near Ciara and that her head was bleeding. Had she ... had she been attacked?"

The old man shrugged. There was a weariness about him. "I can't say with certainty. Perhaps someone struck her. Or perhaps she fell and hit her head while fleeing. We will never know. But that changes nothing. She died as a result of being hunted. Her pursuers assumed you died with her. I had to make certain they kept believing that."

"So you gave me to a woman whose child was stillborn."

The pain of the memory filled his eyes. "I didn't want to, but I had sworn to protect you and that was the surest way."

Maeve stared down at her hands. "Did Bronagh and Eamon know who I was?"

Bradan's shoulders sagged. "Truthfully, I don't know. The woman was unconscious when we made the exchange, but as I stole away into the trees with the dead child, I thought I saw a man standing at the entrance to an outbuilding. I'm fairly certain it was the blacksmith, Eamon. If he had seen the exchange, he may have told his wife. I don't know. Neither of them has ever spoken to me of it—and they have had many opportunities."

Maeve frowned. "What do you mean?"

"I didn't abandon you, Maeve," the old man said. "I had to entrust the blacksmith and his wife with your care, but I followed your progress—from the safety of distance. I urged the Druid masters to work with their apprentices in the forest near your village each summer. Though I had no student of my own, I accompanied the group under the pretext of offering my services as a seer to the local folk. In truth, I was there to check on you."

"Were you aware of how they treated me?"

He dropped his gaze. "I suspected."

Anger rose in Maeve. "Yet you left me there!"

Bradan's head snapped up. "I could do nothing. In the eyes of the people you were their daughter. By law, I had no claim to you. I had to wait for the right opportunity. When you began showing strong signs of your gift, I knew it was time."

"And what if I hadn't shown signs of my gift?" Maeve demanded. "Would I be there still?" When Bradan didn't answer, she jumped up from the stump and began stomping around the tiny clearing. "You would have left me there," she cried. "I can't believe it. How could you? You say you watched out for me, but what was the good of that? I was beaten almost daily. Do you call that keeping me safe?"

"Maeve, please—"

She shook her head and her eyes flashed fire. "No! I won't listen to your excuses. You only took me away because of my gift. If I weren't a seer you would have left me there forever!"

"That is not true," Bradan protested. "I would have come to you on your fourteenth birth day. I would have told you the truth then and let you make your own choice. I swear."

But Maeve was beyond hearing. She shot the old Druid a murderous glare and stormed away.

Chapter 8

Maeve had much to think about. She felt betrayed; Bradan had abandoned her. But as furious as she was with him, her heart knew he was a good man. From the first time she'd met him, he'd made her feel safe. He'd left her with horrible people, but there was no way he could have known, and the urgency of the situation left him no opportunity to find out. And as awful as her life had been, Maeve had survived. When it came down to it, Bradan had kept his promise to Ciara.

That didn't keep Maeve from feeling cheated and ill-used. She'd been made to feel stupid, useless and unloved her whole life. She would carry those feelings and memories with her always.

Maeve had been walking in circles while she sorted her thoughts, but as her emotions started to settle and she began to focus on the story of her birth and her mother's death, her feet turned her toward the forest.

Now that she thought about it, Bradan had actually told her very little. She had more questions than ever. What had Ciara been like? Why had she been hunted?

It occurred to Maeve that she must have other family too. If she had a mother, she must also have a father. And what about her grandparents? Bradan had said they were also seers. What had happened to them? Maeve's fingers instinctively reached for the crystal at her throat. Perhaps it would help her find answers.

She set off for the Bridge of Whispers.

She hadn't even reached the forest when a voice behind her called, "Hold up!"

Maeve spun around, her plans forgotten.

"Declan!" She peered past him. "Don't you have lessons?"

"I did." He grinned. "Until Bradan talked to Finn."

Maeve couldn't help wondering what he'd said. "Finn let you go?"

"He did."

"I wonder why."

Declan shrugged. "He didn't say. And I didn't ask. I was just glad for a free afternoon. And since you have one as well"—he waggled his eyebrows—"I thought we might do something together."

Maeve clapped her hands. "I can think of nothing better. What should we do?"

"For a start, we should get far from the Ruin before someone finds work for us."

"You're right," Maeve agreed, and the two started to run.

But instead of continuing to the forest, Declan led her down the meadow and past the pond.

"Where are we going?" she said when they finally slowed to a walk.

He pointed to the woodland in the distance.

"Oh, good," she said. "I love being among the trees."

"I know, but that's not why we're going."

"It isn't?" Maeve eyed him curiously. "Why then?"

"To see the sea."

"The sea is in the forest?"

"No." He chuckled. "But there is a magnificent view of it. The trees open onto a small clearing in one spot, and the sea is everywhere you look. One day when we have more time we'll go to the sea itself—it's not that far—but for now we can enjoy the view."

Maeve smiled happily. "I've always loved the sea. It's quite near where I grew up, and I would often go with—my mother." She almost choked on the word but didn't want to refer to Bronagh by name lest it prompt Declan to ask questions. "She took Deirdre and me along to carry the eggs she sold there."

"Well then, you're certain to like this."

They continued on their way, chatting easily as they tramped through the long grass.

"What were you planning to do just now if I hadn't come along?" Declan asked.

"Go to the forest," Maeve replied, and they both laughed. "I was going to work with my pendulum."

"How are you getting on with that?"

"It's a bit early to tell. Bradan has taught me how to use it, but it's up to me to master the skills. So lately my lessons are taken up with the protocol and ethics of pendulums."

"There are rules for using pendulums? And moral conduct?"

"Bradan always impresses upon me that being a seer is not a game, and a seer's tools are not toys. Being a seer is a gift, and with it comes great responsibility."

"It is the same with being a bard. I love learning stories and telling them, but Finn reminds me daily of the importance of getting them right. I mustn't add things or leave details out. I must create images with my words, but at the same time I must be truthful, respectful and sincere."

Maeve touched his arm. "Do you remember last year when I was selling eggs in the village and I said you led an easy life?"

Declan squinted at the sky as he thought. Finally he said, "I believe it was the day I first took you to the Druid camp."

"That's right. It was. Anyway, I was wrong. Being a Druid is much harder than I ever imagined. I'm sorry I made light of it."

He laughed. "No need to apologize. I wasn't bothered. Being a Druid has challenges—that's for certain—but I wouldn't want any other life."

"Nor would I," Maeve agreed.

They'd reached the edge of the forest, and the trees loomed above them as if deciding whether to allow them entry. Declan took Maeve's hand and started in.

As she followed the meandering path he carved around trees and bushes, she breathed in the earthy smells and opened her ears to the woodland sounds.

It wasn't a part of the forest that she was accustomed to, and though she couldn't say what, something was different. Something wasn't right. Probably its nearness to the sea, she decided as the pungent, briny scent of it invaded her senses.

"We're almost there," Declan said a moment later.

Then they were through the last of the trees and standing on a narrow strip of grass overlooking a steep bank. Stretching before her as far as she could see—just as Declan had promised—was the sea and the sky.

She breathed in the delicious air until she was sure her lungs would burst. It was glorious. The afternoon breeze had braided the smells of the sea and forest together. They whirled and spun through her body and she felt the wonder of them all the way to her toes. She looked up. Squawking gulls glided and reeled above the glittering sea.

After a time, she looked down. "Oh my! The bank is very steep, isn't it?" She eyed the outcropping of rock. "I certainly wouldn't want to go for a tumble. It's quite lovely though," she added, taking in the lush patches of grass and wildflowers.

"That's why I like it here. No matter the season, it's always peacefully beautiful."

"It truly is," Maeve agreed. And then, "Oh, Declan, look!"

"What?"

Maeve pointed to a vibrant splotch of purple partway down the bank. "It's sea aster! I'm sure of it."

"Pretty," he said.

"It's wonderful for eating. I've collected it often, though it's a bit early for it to be blooming. I've only ever found sea aster in the salt marshes, but I've heard of it growing on cliffs." She grinned at him. "Cara would be thrilled if we brought some back—she might even smile. Let's climb down and pick a bunch."

Declan looked skeptical. "If we lost our footing, we could end up bouncing off boulders all the way to the bottom."

Maeve rolled her eyes. "It's not that dangerous."

"That's not what you said a minute ago."

"I hadn't really looked then," she said. "And anyway, the flowers aren't too far down the bank. We're young and nimble. We'll be fine."

"I'll tell you what. There's no sense both of us risking injury. I'll climb down and get the flowers. You wait here."

Maeve started to object but then stopped. The expression on Declan's face left no doubt that this was as close as she was going to get to having her way.

"Be careful," she said as he started down the bank.

Despite her insistence that the slope wasn't dangerous, Maeve held her breath as Declan began his descent. Seeing him wedge his feet into the slope and hang on to the grass for balance, she realized the bank was steep indeed. She began to regret pressuring him to attempt it. Finally he reached the clump of sea asters and—hanging on to a boulder with one hand—picked the flowers. Maeve would have cheered him on, but she didn't want to distract him. He still had to climb back up.

She sidestepped her way across the clearing until she was directly above him. The least she could do was give him a hand up when he got near the top.

With her gaze fixed on the ground, she inched forward, and then—suddenly—she was over the edge.

She screamed and hit the ground so hard the air rushed from her lungs.

Thud. Bump, bump, bump. She began to tumble down the bank.

The ground was harder than it looked, even without encountering any rocks. She was moving quickly, and yet it felt like time had stopped. She could see everything before it happened. In another moment she would crash directly into Declan and the cluster of boulders beside him. That would likely kill them both.

Acting on instinct, she twisted her body so she rolled to the right. She couldn't slow herself down, but at least she wouldn't collide with Declan.

A mass of boulders rose up in front of her. They were too close to avoid. Maeve squeezed her eyes shut and waited for the impact that would surely kill her. And then the bottom fell out of her stomach. Instead of crashing into the rocks, she dropped into a gully in front of them.

Woomph!

Once again the breath was pushed from her lungs.

"Maeve! Maeve!" It was Declan.

She gulped for air. She didn't want him to panic and risk his own safety. "I'm fine," she gasped, hoping that was the truth. She tested her body. All her parts seemed to work.

"Stay where you are," he said. "I'm coming to you."

By the time he arrived, Maeve had righted herself. Declan still held the bouquet of sea asters, and her heart tightened in her chest.

"What happened?" he asked, his face awash with concern.

"I don't know," she replied, though it was a lie.

She looked toward the clifftop. Grass, trees and sky—that was all. But it changed nothing. As sure as she was sitting in the gully, she knew her fall hadn't been an accident. She hadn't tripped or slipped. She hadn't lost her balance.

She'd been pushed.

With Declan's hand supporting her back, Maeve dragged herself onto the ledge. Then she flopped down on the grass and stared up at the sky.

Declan stretched out beside her. "Are you sure you're all right?"

She turned her head so that they lay staring at one another. "A few scratches and bruises, but otherwise I'm fine."

"You were very lucky."

"I know. You were right. Picking the sea asters was a bad idea."

Declan reached into the inner pocket of his mantle and pulled out the sad-looking bunch of flowers.

Despite the situation, Maeve giggled.

"How did you fall?" Declan asked.

She sobered. "I'm not sure."

In truth, she was absolutely sure. Even now, she could feel hands on her back. She shuddered at the memory, then pulled herself up to a sitting position and looked around. Not that she expected to see anyone. Whoever had sent her over the ledge would be long gone.

She considered telling Declan her suspicions but rejected the idea. He would think she had imagined it. How could someone have pushed her? There was no one here but them.

Maeve shrugged off the incident as carelessness, but she couldn't stop thinking about it. She wasn't even able to keep up a conversation during the walk back to the Ruin. Someone had wanted to hurt her—perhaps kill her! But who? And why?

Maeve asked Declan not to mention her fall. Since she hadn't been hurt, there was no point making a fuss. Even so, the evening meal was a trial. Maeve was preoccupied and it showed.

"Do your ears need cleaning, my girl?" Cara scolded her during the washing-up. "This is the third time I've asked you for more hot water."

"Sorry, Cara," Maeve muttered and hurried away to fill the pot. As she passed Bradan, she felt his gaze on her and knew he suspected something. She gave him a wide berth for the remainder of the evening.

When she finally escaped to her pallet, she pulled the coverlet tight to her chin. No amount of thinking was going to tell her who had pushed her—or why. But one thing was certain: from now on, she would be on her guard.

Chapter 9

It was the eve of Imbolc. Spring was near, and tomorrow they would celebrate the waning of winter and pay homage to Brighid, goddess of the sun. Already cows' udders were heavy with milk, and soon bawling calves would be cavorting in farmers' fields. Since Imbolc was a celebration for women, the men left things to the females. Preparations began at dawn, and Maeve was so busy she had no time to worry about the previous day's row with Bradan or the incident in the forest.

Cara was in charge, and Maeve went looking for her to be assigned another task. She spied her in front of the Ruin, tying a sheaf of rushes to the lintel above the entrance.

"There," Cara said, stepping back to admire her handiwork. "That should invite Brighid in."

Maeve nodded. "It looks very welcoming." She pointed to the pile of logs by the firepit. "I finished stacking the firewood. What would you like me to do now?"

Cara gestured to the Ruin. "You can help the other women scrub the sleeping chambers. If Brighid is to bless this home, it must be clean."

By the time the Druids gathered for the midday meal, Maeve was already tired, but she was happy for the distraction. The afternoon was more of the same, so when she finally dragged herself to the long, plank tables at the end of the day, she could barely keep her eyes open.

That night she slept like the dead and would have continued to do so long after daybreak if not for Enda.

"Wake up, wake up," her friend laughed as she shook Maeve's shoulder. "You don't want to sleep through Imbolc. The burning of the fields will begin soon. We have to hurry."

Maeve rolled from her pallet and dressed with her eyes closed, reluctant to leave the oblivion of sleep. "Did Brighid come?" she mumbled as she pulled on her robe.

"She must have," Enda replied brightly. "Last night Cara scattered a layer of white ash over the ground in front of the entrance to the Ruin, and this morning she found a woman's footprints." She passed Maeve her mantle. "Brighid must have come during the night and blessed the clothes and other belongings we left out."

Maeve and Enda took their places along the long edge of the field with the village women, farmers' wives and other Druidesses. Dressed in robes of white, red and black, the women raised their torches high and waited for the blessing. When it came, they lowered their torches to the stubbled field and began burning their way across. Soaked by the morning mist, the ground smoked more than flamed, but when Maeve looked back, it was black all the same. It was ready for the spring planting. The women moved on to the next field and others after that. When they were done, they built a mighty fire and shared a meal of milk, bread, cheese and dried berries in honour of Brighid.

As the Druid women returned to the Ruin, they chatted excitedly about the evening feast—a pig and several quail were to be roasted over a spit and served with onions, turnip and squash. Though she had just eaten, Maeve's mouth watered at the prospect.

She listened contentedly as the women discussed their plans. The day had been charged with energy and camaraderie, something she had never before experienced. She had taken part in Imbolc celebrations before, but she couldn't remember them ever being fun. Her mother—no, she must stop thinking of Bronagh that way—Bronagh had a way of sucking the enjoyment out of everything.

Maeve wondered what it would have been like sharing Imbolc with Ciara. Bradan had said she brought joy wherever she went. How Maeve would have liked to know her.

The crystal at her neck grew warm, catching her by surprise. Her pendulum wanted to tell her something. She was sure of it. Her sense of peace vanished, and she was overwhelmed by an urgent need to get away.

She tugged on Enda's sleeve. "There's something I must do. I shall meet up with you at the Ruin."

"But—" Enda began.

"I'll be back in time to help with the feast, I promise."

And without another word Maeve bounded for the forest, not stopping until she reached the stream. As she stood on the bridge, catching her breath, she took the pendulum from her neck and held it in her palm. Its warmth pulsed in time with her beating heart.

"I know you want to tell me something," she whispered, "but how do I know what to ask?"

As Maeve mulled over the possibilities, she held out her arm. When the crystal became still, she offered the blessing and established the pendulum's intentions. It was ready. If only she knew what to ask.

Maeve sensed the right question was somewhere inside her mind. She had only to find it. In the past she would have become frustrated with such a dilemma. But today was different. She and the crystal were one. If it had the answer, she was confident she had the question. She reminded herself of Bradan's teachings—observe, sense, think and weigh the findings. If she did those things, the truth would become clear.

She closed her eyes and saw herself walking back to the Ruin with the other Druid women and thinking this was the first time she'd enjoyed Imbolc. Then her thoughts had shifted to her resentment of Bronagh for always turning things sour, and that led her to wonder how life might have been different if she'd grown up with her real mother.

And that's when the crystal had become warm.

It knew more about her mother—and it wanted to tell her.

Maeve's thoughts drifted back to the day she'd found it. Even as her fingers had closed around it in the frigid stream, it had felt warm. It was as if they were meant for each other. With so many stones to choose from, it was a wonder Maeve had ever found it. Except the copper-haired young woman had drawn her to it.

Maeve knew what to ask.

She steadied her arm and said, "Pendulum, is Ciara the young woman I keep seeing at the Bridge of Whispers?" She held her breath.

The pendulum began circling.

Yes. Yes! Yes, yes, yes!

Maeve realized that deep within her heart, she'd always known the woman at the bridge was her mother.

An ache welled up in her chest. She longed for the mother she'd never known. Ciara's death should never have happened.

It was as if her blood had caught fire, and as it

coursed through her body her entire being burned with rage. She couldn't think. She willed herself to calm. She mustn't let her emotions get the better of her. Maeve took several cleansing breaths, and when she was once more in control of her mind, she turned to her pendulum. "Do you know who is responsible for my mother's death?" It wasn't the question she wanted to ask—it didn't provide her with names—but it was all she could think of.

Maeve stared at her pendulum, but it didn't move. She repeated the question. No response. Not even a perhaps. When she asked a third time and still received no answer, she dropped her arm. The pendulum was not going to speak to her.

Maeve wanted to scream and kick something. No matter which way she turned, she kept bumping into walls that stopped her from moving forward.

She pushed her emotions back into place. Throwing a fit wouldn't help. She would think more about this later. Now she must get back to the Ruin. She slipped the chain over her head and turned to leave.

And there—at the edge of the forest—stood Ciara. At her feet was a small, bright fire. She lowered herself to it and beckoned Maeve to join her. When Maeve hunkered down beside her, Ciara looked as if she wanted to touch Maeve, but after a time she turned her gaze to the flames. She stared at the fire so long and so intently that Maeve finally looked into it too.

At first all she saw were fiery tendrils licking the air, but then within the flames a shimmering image took shape. As her eyes adjusted to the dancing lights and shadows, she realized she was looking at the Great Hall of Castle Carrick. It was just as it had been when she and Bradan had gone there for the council of war—banners lining the walls, and kings and chieftains shouting.

Then the flames flickered and the image changed. Now Maeve was looking into a single face. Icy grey eyes glared at her from inside the fire. Maeve's heart jumped within her chest, just as it had when Queen Ailsa had stared her down at the council of war. Even from across the crowded room, the woman's gaze had paralyzed her.

She turned away quickly and looked at her mother.

Ciara was no longer smiling. "Beware," she whispered gravely. Then she disappeared.

Chapter 10

"No!" Maeve reached for Ciara, but her fingers closed on air. "Come back. Please." But the place where her mother had been remained empty.

Maeve buried her face in her hands. It was too much. The last few days had been an emotional storm. When she'd learned to use her pendulum, she was hopeful she would find the answers she had been seeking and her life would begin to make sense.

Her discovery that she was a Druid came at the cost of knowing her life as the blacksmith's daughter had been a lie. And though her true mother had been revealed to her, she was dead and lost to Maeve forever. Each time something was given to her, something else was taken away. It was more than she could bear.

Maeve gave in to her despair and began to cry inconsolably, screaming her frustration to the wind. When she was finally out of tears, she swiped at her wet face with her sleeve.

Maybe there were no answers, she thought miserably. Maybe life was nothing but questions. Maybe she would never truly know who she was.

From the corner of her eye, she became aware of a yellow glow and turned to see her mother's fire still burning. It burned without wood. There were no logs, no kindling, no ash. Why hadn't she noticed those things before?

She passed her hand through the flame. It should have burned her, but it didn't. There was no heat at all. It was the ghost of a fire, just as her mother was the ghost of a woman. The thought threatened another wave of tears, but Maeve fought them back.

She knew her mother must have left the fire here for a reason. As Maeve stared at it, she allowed her eyes to glaze over and her gaze to sway with the flames.

That's all that was needed to convince the fire to reveal its secrets. The piercing grey eyes of Queen Ailsa once again glared at Maeve from its depths, and once again her heart skipped a beat. But as she watched, the image of the queen became a castle chamber where the queen was sharing tea and conversation with Ciara.

Maeve blinked in disbelief, but before she could ponder what she was seeing, the scene changed again. Now she was staring into her mother's kind and concerned face, warning her to beware.

Then the fire disappeared too. Maeve touched the ground where it had been, but there was only grass.

She was confused. The fire showed her mother being friendly with the queen, yet she was warning Maeve against her. True, the queen bore Maeve no love. Not after her interpretation of the king's dream had undone the queen's plans and exposed her betrayal. But that wasn't enough. A piece of the story was missing.

Maeve's thoughts kept returning her to Castle Carrick for the council of war. Before that day she had never met Queen Ailsa—never even laid eyes on her. But the loathing in the woman's stare from across the Great Hall had pierced Maeve as surely as a marksman's arrow. There was no denying the queen's hatred. The mere memory made Maeve shudder.

But why should the queen despise her so then? Before the council of war Queen Ailsa hadn't even known Maeve existed. Bradan had said the queen was not fond of Druids, but the look she'd sent Maeve went beyond that.

Maeve tried to push aside thoughts of the queen. Even if she did hate Maeve, she was locked away in a castle in the North Country.

And yet Maeve couldn't dismiss Ciara's warning or the image of the queen and her mother in friendly conversation. The two things didn't fit.

The quartz crystal at her throat began to pulse with warmth.

Of course! She loosened the chain from her neck and stood up. She dangled the chain from her fingers until the crystal became still. "Pendulum," she said, "am I in danger from the queen?"

The crystal began to swing in a wide circle, more emphatically than it ever had before. "Oh, no," she gasped, clutching the crystal to her breast. Its confirmation of Ciara's warning shook Maeve to her core.

Once again she felt herself being pushed off the edge of the hill overlooking the sea. Her life was truly in danger.

Maeve smelled the roasting pig before she came in sight of the Ruin. It made her mouth water, but it also pricked her with guilt. She had promised to help with the feast, and she had broken her word. She quickened her step.

"Maeve! Where have you been?" asked Enda. "Are you all right? You look like you've been crying."

Maeve forced a smile. "I'm fine. A bug flew into my eye, and now it won't stop watering."

Enda nodded, apparently satisfied with the explanation. "We're about to take the pig off the spit. Could you drain the vegetables?"

Maeve forced another smile. "Of course."

She got straight to work, being careful to save the liquid from the turnips and squash. Cara would want it for soup.

At last the meal was ready, and with great good humour the Druids sat down to eat. It was a more raucous meal than Maeve could ever recall. There was much talking and laughter, as well as numerous blessings of Brighid and toasts to the women and the fine bounty they had set forth.

When everyone had eaten and the cleanup was done, the Druids gathered around the fire and Finn treated them to a tale of Imbolc past. Finn was a wonderful storyteller, but Maeve was too preoccupied to focus on his story.

A hand on her shoulder pulled her from her thoughts. When she turned to see who it was, Bradan crooked a finger, gesturing her away from the fire.

Curious, Maeve slipped from her place and followed him into the shadow of the Ruin. The two hadn't spoken since their quarrel. Perhaps Bradan wanted to apologize.

"So how was your first Imbolc as a Druid?" he asked when they were well away from the others.

Was this why he had called her from the fire? Surely he could have asked that at their morning lesson. After more thought she decided perhaps it was his way of moving past the awkwardness between them.

"It was good," she said. "I enjoyed it more than the other Imbolc celebrations I've been part of. I felt connected to the women—and to Brighid. The day had more meaning than it has in the past."

"I thought you might say that," he replied. "After all, being born on Imbolc links you to Brighid herself. And this particular Imbolc marks your entry into womanhood. Today you are a child no more."

Maeve opened her mouth to tell Bradan he'd got it wrong. She'd been born the day after Imbolc. But then she realized he was right. She wasn't sure how to feel about that. She'd been robbed of her real birth day her whole life. But at the same time the discovery excited her, as if being born on this celebration day made her special. It was a baseless notion, yet it comforted her.

Bradan broke into her thoughts. "I have a favour to ask. I am in need of some things from the village, and I fear I am not yet hale enough to make the journey myself. I wonder if you could get them for me. I understand Enda is going there tomorrow. Perhaps you could accompany her."

Maeve nodded. "Of course."

"Thank you."

Maeve bobbed her head and turned back toward the fire, but Bradan put a hand on her arm to stop her.

"There is one more thing," he said as he pressed something heavy and cold into her hand. "I have a gift for you."

It was a ring. Maeve could barely make it out in the dim light—hammered silver with some sort of burnished design.

Was this meant as a peace offering? "It's a man's ring."

"A man's pinky ring," he said. "I think it should fit nicely on your thumb."

Maeve slid it on. Bradan was right. It fit perfectly. "But why are you giving it to me?"

He covered her hands with his. "It was always meant for you, Maeve. I've simply been waiting for this day to give it to you. Never be parted from it. When the time comes to use it, you will know."

Chapter 11

It had been a long day and Maeve was weary to her bones. Even so, when she crawled into bed, her mind refused to settle. She had no idea who had pushed her, but she was certain Queen Ailsa was behind it. Though locked away in the North Country, she was still a threat. She might not be able to leave her castle prison, but she had minions aplenty who could do her bidding.

Once more Maeve's thoughts returned to her almost fatal fall and she shuddered. Someone had definitely pushed her. She didn't want to believe it was anyone she knew. But she hadn't seen any strangers lurking about either. Someone had been spying on her. And since she and Declan hadn't told anyone where they were going that day, whoever it was must have followed them.

If Maeve's would-be killer knew he had failed, would he try again? With that worrisome question circling her brain, Maeve fell into a troubled sleep.

Her body jerked her awake. Her skin was damp with sweat and she was shivering. She pulled the coverlet to her chin and stared into the darkness, waiting for her heart to cease pounding and her breathing to slow.

It had happened again. Her resting mind had told her what her active mind could not, just as it had when she'd solved Bradan's riddle. But this time Maeve had been asleep when it happened. Asleep and dreaming. In the dream, she was staring at the fire Ciara had conjured and Queen Ailsa was glaring at her. Maeve's gaze was locked with the queen's as if by magic. A current of energy joined them, and all the queen's hatred ran along it and poured into Maeve like poison.

Then, as with Ciara's fire, Maeve suddenly found herself staring at her mother and the queen drinking tea and talking. This time, though, the queen's pleasant expression turned thunderous and she sprang from her chair, pointed at Ciara's belly and cried, "A child for a child."

The words—like a chant—echoed inside Maeve's head, getting louder and louder until she'd been jolted from her sleep.

What did it mean—a child for a child?

Ciara had warned her to beware of the queen. Bradan said Maeve had been in danger from the moment she was born. He had feared Ciara's enemies would harm her as they had her mother. A child for a child. The queen had repeated it over and over in Maeve's dream. Was Queen Ailsa responsible for Ciara's death? Did she hate Maeve because she was Ciara's child?

Maeve pressed her hands over her ears to block out the queen's voice.

For the remainder of the night, Maeve tossed and turned and worried.

When she joined the other Druids for the morning meal, she was a jumble of nerves. It was little wonder she jumped when Enda reached across her for the honey pot.

"What's gotten into you?" her friend asked. "You're as jittery as a mouse in a cottage of cats."

"I'm fine." Maeve forced an anaemic smile. "You startled me is all. I was thinking about something."

"Never mind that now. We need to be on our way if we're going to get to the village before the crowd. Eat your gruel and let's be off."

Maeve had forgotten about the outing. She picked up her spoon, dug into her porridge—and then stopped. What if the gruel had been poisoned? She looked around the table at the others hungrily cleaning their bowls. Everyone's porridge had come from the same pot, she reasoned, lifting the spoon to her mouth. She sniffed it and then furtively studied the people around her. Were they watching her? No. They were all simply filling their bellies. Maeve silently scolded herself. She was letting her fears get the better of her. No one at the Ruin would do her harm. And yet …

She dropped her spoon back into the bowl and stood up. "I'm not hungry," she told Enda. "Let us go."

By the time they reached the road leading to

the village, Maeve's common sense had pushed back her fears. She couldn't spend every minute avoiding people and imagining the worst. She wouldn't feel safe anywhere. If she kept her eyes and ears open and stayed close to those she trusted, she would be fine.

The market was in the centre of the village where the main roads converged, and by the time Maeve and Enda arrived, most of the vendors had already set out their wares. There were stalls boasting colourful bolts of cloth and others offering stacks of baskets and bowls. There were tanners selling hides beside farmers and fishmongers. Candlemakers lured passersby with promises of enduring light, and confectioners shouted the delectability of their sweets while shooing away children trying to help themselves to samples.

Sellers hawking charms, roasted chestnuts and bunches of herbs walked among the crowd and waved their wares under buyers' noses. It reminded Maeve of when she'd spent afternoons selling eggs.

The two young women got to work hunting down the items they'd come for. Within half an hour they had everything they needed. With no other pressing business, they began a second, more leisurely stroll through the market.

The square was now quite crowded. It was a sunny morning and some of the vendors had erected awnings to provide shade and further mark the boundaries of their space. Maeve and Enda wandered in and around them all.

"Oh, look." Enda pointed to a silversmith forging a chain. Bright cloth laid on the ground in front of him showed off jewelry, goblets, platters, clasps and buckles. "Let's watch him work."

Maeve nodded and they jostled their way into a small group admiring his wares. Maeve had seen her father—no, not her father, Eamon the blacksmith—shape tools and harness at his forge many a time, but the work of a silversmith was much more delicate. For several minutes the man grew the silver chain as the throng looked on, but eventually he put down his small hammer and attempted to entice onlookers to part with a few of their coins.

He was an older fellow—probably of an age with Bradan—but clean-shaven, save for a few days' stubble. His face was leathery and rutted with heavy lines that deepened when he smiled. His hair was a scant wisp of white.

He grinned at a woman browsing the silver trinkets. "I know just what you need, mistress," he said, snatching up a silver comb and holding it out for her. "Hair as fine as yours is begging for a comb such as this."

When the woman shook her head and moved on, the old silversmith turned his attention to others in the crowd. A few were convinced to make purchases, but most carried on to other vendors.

Having lost interest, Enda grabbed Maeve's arm and began tugging her toward another stall where a severe-looking woman stood waving. "It's Una," she told Maeve.

"Who is Una?" Maeve dug in her heels. She wanted to browse more of the silversmith's work.

Enda clucked her tongue. "I told you about her—don't you remember? She's here from the Midlands, visiting her brother. She's ever so nice. Come. I want you to meet her." When Maeve continued to resist, Enda huffed in exasperation, "What's the matter with you, girl? Lift your feet. You walk like you have an anvil in each boot."

Maeve sighed and clomped after her friend.

While the two women exchanged greetings, Maeve glanced around the stall. It was brimming with iron pots and cauldrons of all sizes scattered over the ground and stacked in tall, wobbly piles. The pots put her in mind of the ones used at the Ruin. It struck Maeve as odd that she'd never before considered where such pots came from. All she knew was that every household had them—usually several.

She heard her name and forced her mind back to the market.

"And this is my friend," Enda said.

"Hello." Maeve bobbed her head.

"Nice to meet you," Una replied. She was smiling, but Maeve thought it looked as if the effort pained her. The woman's mouth was stretched so tight across her hollow cheeks it looked like her skin might rip. "Enda has told me much about you."

"Really?" Maeve cast a surprised glance in her friend's direction.

"Oh my, yes. She says you interpreted the Great King's dream and saved everyone in the land."

"I fear she made more of the matter than needs be," Maeve said. She would have to speak to Enda about her penchant for gossip. Some things were better kept private. Maeve changed the subject. "Enda says you are visiting your brother. Is he here with you?"

"Uh, no. I've come alone. He's busy with his farm, and I wanted to see what the market was like."

Enda laughed. "What are you talking about, Una? You've been to the market before. This is where we met."

Una laughed nervously. "Yes, yes. I know. I meant that I wanted to see if there were different vendors than the last time I came. And there are." She held her hands palm up to indicate the stall they were in. "This pot seller wasn't here before."

"Are you looking to buy a pot?" Maeve asked.

"Perhaps," Una replied. "My brother could use another. It's just a matter of finding the right size." She began wandering toward the stacks, so Enda and Maeve followed.

"How big does it need be?" Enda asked. Una formed a circle with her arms and Enda gazed upward.

"There's one like that up there." She pointed. "The question is how to get it."

"Perhaps the pot vendor can get it for you," Maeve said, but Una had wandered around to the other side of the stack.

Suddenly there was a mighty grumbling of iron rubbing on iron, and Maeve watched in horror as the pile of black pots and cauldrons began to teeter.

"Look out!" Enda shouted.

Chapter 12

Trying to get out of the way, Maeve stepped backward into another stack of pots, setting them teetering too, and a medium-sized kettle toppled from the top. She was able to bat it away but lost her balance in the process and down she went. Protecting her head with one arm, she used the other to fend off the pots now raining down. She tried to pull in her legs, but before she could, a large cauldron dropped onto her foot, sending a sharp pain up her leg.

The thunderous avalanche lasted only seconds, but even after the final cauldron hit the ground, Maeve remained perfectly still. The startled onlookers sprang into action, clearing away the debris and helping her to her feet. She flinched as she put weight on her ankle, prompting the pot vendor to fetch a stool.

"Are you all right, lass?" he asked, helping her seat herself and scrutinizing her for further injury. "Nothing like this has ever happened before."

Enda pushed him aside. "Let me through," she said. "I'm a healer."

"It's just my ankle," Maeve assured her.

"And your head." Enda frowned, placing a finger on Maeve's temple.

Maeve winced. "Ow. I don't remember that happening."

"Well it did." Enda was all business. "The skin is split and there's a good-sized bump. You'll likely have a headache and a bruise, but all things considered, it doesn't look too bad. Let me see your leg."

Maeve lifted her robe to the top of her boot.

"Your ankle is already swollen," Enda said, pressing it in several places, causing Maeve to flinch. "I shan't remove your boot or we'll never get it on again. I don't think you've broken any bones, but your foot's had a nasty whack. I'll be able to make better sense of things once we get you to the Ruin. Do you think you can walk?"

As it turned out, Maeve didn't have to. The vendor—no doubt suffering from guilt—took them back in his cart, leaving his son to clean up the mess and deal with customers.

"It happened so fast," Maeve said as they bumped along the dirt road. Her leg was propped on a pile of hay to minimize the jostling. "One minute we were helping Una find a pot, and the next minute entire stacks of them were crashing down on me." She regarded Enda curiously. "Speaking of Una, whatever happened to her? She just disappeared. After she went around to the back of the pots I never saw her again."

Enda cocked her head in thought. "Come to

think on it, nor did I. Not even after the pots fell. It's odd. The racket brought everyone else in the market running." She shrugged. "Perhaps we didn't see her for the crowd."

"Perhaps," Maeve murmured, though she wasn't convinced. Her eyes narrowed. "What do you know about Una?"

Her friend answered warily. "Why are you asking that?"

Maeve realized her serious tone had startled Enda. The last thing she wanted was to make her defensive. Maeve assumed a disinterested expression and shrugged. "No reason. Talking takes my mind off my ankle is all, and Una seems as good a topic as any."

That seemed to put Enda at ease again. "Well, I've seen her twice before—both times at the market. The first time we literally ran into each other. Both of us dropped our bundles and had to pick them up, so naturally we got to talking. I said as how I hadn't seen her in the village before, and that's when she explained she was from the Midlands."

Maeve nodded. "She certainly had a Midlands accent. The servants at Castle Carrick had the same manner of speaking." Castle Carrick, home of King Owen, brother of Queen Ailsa. That is where the queen would have grown up. She probably knew most everyone there. "Is she married?" Maeve asked. "Does she have children?"

Enda mumbled, "I don't believe she said."

"Why is she visiting her brother?"

"She didn't tell me that either." Enda was beginning to look flustered. She offered Maeve a nervous smile. "Does a sister need a reason to visit her brother?"

Maeve didn't relent. "Who is her brother? What is his name?"

"She didn't say."

"It seems Una didn't say a great deal about anything," Maeve observed and then added, "Too bad the same can't be said of you."

Enda's mouth dropped open. "And what do you mean by that, may I ask?" The indignation in her voice was unmistakable.

"Una seemed to know a great deal about me."

"Well, she asked, didn't she!" Enda retorted.

"Why though? I'm nobody to her. How did I come up in your conversation?"

"The woman was just friendly," Enda said defensively. "She said she could see that I was a Druid and she'd heard there was a young seer in our midst. A pretty ginger-haired lass, she said. I told her we were friends. I only said good things about you—never once mentioned your stubborn streak nor how you are short on patience—so you needn't worry that I've sullied your name."

"You told her I interpreted King Redmond's dream. What else did you tell her?"

"As I said, nothing terrible. I told her how you were apprenticing with Bradan and how you were a creature of the forest. Mostly that was all."

Maeve's heart began to thud in her chest. That was enough.

When they reached the Ruin, the pot vendor—a burly fellow—carried Maeve to a bench at one of the tables and deposited a large cauldron beside the fire pit as compensation for the accident. Then he apologized one more time and headed back to the village.

A cart's appearance was unusual at the Ruin, and curiosity pulled the Druids from their work. Soon a large group had gathered around Maeve.

"Give me space to tend the girl," Enda grumbled as she pushed through with her bundle of medical supplies.

"What happened?" Declan demanded, hurrying to Maeve's side.

"Just a small accident. A stack of pots fell on me at the market," Maeve said, "but I'm fine."

"Hold your foot still so I can wrap it," Enda commanded.

"You had another accident? Maeve, you have to be more careful."

She shot Declan a warning look. "You agreed not to mention that."

Bradan pushed through the crowd and came to a stop in front of Maeve. "You had another accident recently?" He looked as concerned as Declan.

"It was nothing," Maeve insisted. "I tumbled

down a hill. I wasn't even hurt. I knew you would make a fuss. That's why I asked Declan to keep quiet about it."

Enda finished with Maeve's ankle and stood up. "If you want the swelling to go down, you must try not to walk any more than necessary. Keep your foot up if you can." Then she turned and shooed away the curious spectators. When everyone had left except Declan and Bradan, Enda turned to the lad. "Maeve could use a good walking stick. Can I leave it to you to find her one?"

Declan seemed unsure and glanced at Maeve. When she nodded, he looked relieved and said, "Yes, Enda. Right away," and jogged off toward the wood.

"I'll make you some soothing tea," Enda said and left to heat the water.

Bradan shuffled to the end of the bench and sat down, avoiding Maeve's injured foot. When he was settled, he said, "Your spill down the hill and the pots falling on you—were they accidents?"

That caught Maeve by surprise. But she was relieved to have someone to talk to about her fears, and she was coming to realize this was a problem she should not try to solve alone. "I don't know for certain—I haven't had a chance to ask my pendulum. I suspect someone has been trying"—she paused—"to hurt me."

"I thought as much, though the accidents in themselves aren't sufficient proof. What makes you suspicious?"

"A number of things. A few days ago Declan took me to the eastern wood to view the sea."

Bradan nodded.

"As soon as we stepped into the forest, something felt wrong," Maeve said and recounted the rest of the story.

When she got to the part where Declan climbed down the cliff to get sea asters, Bradan raised a disapproving eyebrow.

Maeve rolled her eyes. "He didn't like the idea either, but he said he'd go if I promised to stay where I was."

"At least the lad has sense," Bradan mumbled.

Maeve ignored the insinuation. "But as I stood watching him, I felt hands on my back and suddenly I was tumbling down the slope."

Bradan eyed her with concern. "Are you saying you were pushed?"

Maeve nodded.

"You could have been killed."

"I think that was the idea. Someone must have been spying on me, and when Declan and I headed down the meadow, that person followed us, hidden in the trees. That's probably the presence I felt in the forest."

"And today?"

"Enda introduced me to a woman she'd met in the market. Her name was Una and she claimed to be visiting her brother. Her manner of speech was very like that of the servants at Castle Carrick.

"I sensed something strange about her from the very start. She seemed to be lying about why she was there, and she knew a lot about me. Admittedly, Enda had told her much of that, but she had known of me before meeting Enda. The most suspicious part, though, is that she disappeared behind the stack of cauldrons just before they fell on me." Maeve shrugged. "We didn't see her again after that."

"And you think she is responsible for the pots falling?"

"I'm certain of it."

The old man cocked his head curiously. "Why would she do that?"

Maeve hesitated. Should she tell Bradan what she knew? She hated keeping secrets from him. But one truth would lead to another and she would likely end up telling him about her encounters with Ciara. She didn't want to share that. Still, there was so much more she needed to know—things only Bradan could tell her. "I think Una pushed me down the slope. When that didn't work, she tried to bury me under an avalanche of iron pots."

"But why?" Bradan asked again.

"I believe she is Queen Ailsa's servant, and the queen wants me dead."

"Who told you this?" he demanded. "Who have you been speaking to?"

Maeve's hand automatically drifted to the crystal at her throat. "My pendulum."

Chapter 13

Bradan's eyebrows dove together. "Your pendulum cannot tell you names."

"I know that," Maeve said.

Bradan looked bewildered. It wasn't a look Maeve had often seen on him. "But how could you know what to ask?" When Maeve didn't reply, his voice softened. "How can I help if you won't tell me what you know, child?"

Maeve scowled. "I am not a child. I am fourteen—old enough to marry if I choose. Yet you treat me as if I was five."

Maeve expected him to scold her for being disrespectful. Instead he said, "I'm sorry. Sometimes I don't see what my eyes show me."

Maeve immediately regretted chastising her mentor. "You have taught me well. Your insistence that I work things out for myself has made me fairly adept at solving problems. On my own I've learned that someone—probably on behalf of the queen—is trying to kill me." She touched the quartz at her throat. "My pendulum has been a great help. But it can tell me only so much."

Enda appeared with two bowls of tea. If she

had heard any of the conversation, she didn't let on. She simply placed the tea on the table and left.

When she was out of earshot, Maeve stared steadily at Bradan and said, "Only you know the whole story."

His gaze didn't waver. "I said I would tell you and so I shall. There was no point before. You wouldn't have believed me. But now that you have assured yourself that I am being honest with you…" He lifted his shoulders in a resigned shrug. Then he reached for the bowls of tea, passing one to Maeve. "First let us drink our tea. Enda said it is soothing."

"My mother has appeared to me several times," Maeve said the instant the old Druid put down his empty bowl. "Though I didn't know that's who I saw until the day of Imbolc."

"Ciara came to you?"

Maeve nodded. "At the Bridge of Whispers."

"She had likely been waiting some time for you to come to her."

Maeve regarded him curiously. "What do you mean?"

"The Bridge of Whispers is where those from the Otherworld can communicate with the living. It is a bridge between the worlds. Remember I told you life is a cycle? When we die in this world, we are born again in the Otherworld, and when we die there, we are reborn in this world. And so it goes."

Maeve did remember, and though it had been an interesting notion, it hadn't seemed important at the time. Now it was. It meant her mother wasn't really lost to her; she was merely somewhere else. If Maeve needed her, she could go to the Bridge of Whispers. It was a great comfort.

Then Maeve had another thought. She frowned.

"What is it?" Bradan asked.

"Why have I never seen anyone else at the bridge? Don't others contact loved ones there?"

He shook his head. "Only seers hear the whispers. To others the bridge is naught but a stone walkway leading nowhere."

If only they knew, Maeve thought, grateful beyond words to have this link to her mother.

Bradan interrupted her reverie. "Tell me more about these encounters."

"I saw her when I was searching for my pendulum. She showed me where to look." Maeve smiled at the memory, and when she glanced at Bradan, he was smiling too.

"She would know," he nodded. "The quartz once belonged to her."

"Really?"

"Yes," the old man said. "She found it in that very stream when she was your age. I threw it back after she died."

"So that's how you knew I'd find it there," Maeve said. The stone at her throat pulsed with warmth and she placed her hand over it. She could feel her mother in it and she knew Ciara would always be with her wherever she went. The realization filled her with new confidence.

"It sometimes feels as if my pendulum is trying to tell me things, even without me asking it questions," she said.

Bradan cocked his head. "How so?"

"It becomes warm. Do all pendulums do that?"

Bradan laughed. "It would seem your mother didn't completely leave the quartz. It is her influence you are sensing."

Maeve made a face. "So now I have two mentors—you and my mother?"

"Don't forget yourself." He winked. "That's the most important mentor of all."

Maeve rolled her eyes and continued her tale. When she started to speak about the council of war, Bradan frowned.

"You had an encounter with the queen at the council of war? You never mentioned it."

"There didn't seem a reason. And it wasn't really an encounter—just a look."

"A look?"

"Yes. The queen noticed me at the back of the chamber and glared at me. It was as if she was shooting arrows of hate with her eyes. I couldn't look away. I nearly fell off the bench I was sitting on." Maeve shuddered. "It unsettles me just remembering."

"She must have guessed who you were."

Bradan spoke more to himself than to Maeve. "I have been a fool. I should never have brought you there." He shook his head and regarded Maeve woefully. "You are so much like your mother it is little wonder your presence stirred up the queen's wrath. She would have seen Ciara in you straight away. Your life was in danger from that moment on. I was careless, and because of that you are not safe."

"There's no sense blaming yourself," Maeve said. "The queen would have found out about me eventually. I'm just glad I know her intentions so I can be wary." Her forehead buckled in thought. "I understand that she would hate me for exposing her plot to defeat King Redmond. But why for being Ciara's daughter? Why did she hate Ciara? The night of Imbolc I dreamt of the queen—her face in the fire glaring at me, her piercing eyes refusing to release me. Then the dream changed and she was in a castle with Ciara, drinking tea and talking. They seemed friendly until the queen jumped up and pointed angrily at Ciara. She kept repeating the same words—'A child for a child'—until they were burned into my brain. What does it mean? Do you know?"

Bradan's face paled.

"You do know."

The old man's mouth tightened. He closed his eyes and softly repeated the phrase. "A child for a child." When he reopened his eyes they shone with unshed tears. "It is the revenge she seeks."

Maeve would have pushed him for an explanation, but the Druid women had begun preparing the midday meal, and the area was now bustling with activity. Not wishing to be overheard, the two agreed to resume their conversation in the copse of oak trees after they'd eaten.

Because of her injury, Maeve was relieved of cleanup duties. With the aid of the stick Declan had found, she hobbled to the meeting place to await her teacher.

"I had a feeling you would be here before me," Bradan said when he arrived.

"Considering what you're about to tell me, I think I've been extremely patient."

Bradan looked at her askance and cleared his throat. "I believe I already mentioned how, by the time she was sixteen, Ciara's skills as a seer were sought by royalty. Queen Ailsa was among those who called upon her.

"Ailsa had been wedded to King Redmond for about two years. All who saw the couple together said they were perfectly matched. He was besotted with her, and she seemed equally smitten with him. There were endless whispers, smiles, stolen glances and secret laughter whenever they were in one another's company.

"In light of the queen's recent treachery against the Great King, one could argue that this wedded bliss was an act, but I believe Queen Ailsa truly loved Redmond."

"What caused her feelings to change?"

Bradan shrugged. "The influence of her brother perhaps. King Owen may have convinced her that his claim to the throne—not Redmond's—was the legitimate one. He may have poisoned her mind with his hatred. Or she may have had reasons of her own."

Maeve thought she detected a note of sadness in the old Druid's voice. "You know what those reasons were," she said.

"I have my suspicions, but only the queen can say for certain." He took a deep breath and continued with his story. "Despite the apparent perfection of the union—a love match as well as a melding of the two most important kingdoms in the land—the queen was troubled. After two years of marriage, she still hadn't borne a child. One of the duties of a queen is to provide an heir, and Queen Ailsa had not yet conceived.

"So it was that while the king and queen were wintering in the southern region, she called upon Ciara to determine the cause of the problem and tell her what could be done about it. She might have been more inclined to accept the truth if it had come from me, since my age deemed me venerable. But because of the delicate nature of her inquiry and because she was young, she turned instead to Ciara. Not only was Ciara a woman, but she was also the same age as the queen.

"And she was with child. Perhaps the queen assumed Ciara would have greater insight into such things." Bradan shrugged. "It matters not.

The queen was certain Ciara could help her." There was regret in his voice. "Looking back, I wish the queen had come to me. Those who don't possess the gift of sight can put too much faith in a seer's abilities. And they sometimes expect the impossible."

Though everything had happened many years ago and Maeve already knew the outcome, she found herself listening with clenched fists.

"Ciara told me their first meeting went well. The queen requested her presence at the winter castle, and they shared tea and sweets. Ailsa made sincere inquiries after Ciara's pregnancy and offered good wishes for a smooth birth."

A sense of foreboding spread through Maeve. This was what she'd seen in her dream.

"Then the queen spoke of her own situation. Ciara encouraged the queen to stay hopeful. She told her that having children came less readily for some women than others, and the queen needed to be patient. She bade her wait one or two more cycles, and if she still hadn't conceived, they would look into the matter further. It is the same counsel I would have given the queen, and though she was anxious to have the problem resolved, the queen agreed to bide her time.

"When two more months passed without any change in her condition, the queen again called Ciara to the castle. Ciara said that perhaps the queen's inner self knew the answer and might reveal the truth through a dream. To increase the chances of that happening, Ciara gave the queen a potion to drink before retiring.

"The next day Ciara returned and the queen recounted her dream. Though she didn't let on, Ciara was troubled, for the dream confirmed the queen's fears. She would never give the king a child. There was little doubt about the matter. But Ciara was reluctant to dash the queen's hopes, so she said the dream wasn't conclusive and suggested they seek the truth using a different method.

"That evening Ciara shared her concerns with me. Should she tell the queen the truth or should she say that—with time—the queen would conceive? I reminded her that seers are bound by honesty. She could speak the truth in a way the queen might choose to interpret to her liking, or she could reveal only part of what she knew. But she couldn't knowingly lie."

Maeve felt the weight of Ciara's dilemma. If she attempted to ease the queen's worry, she was betraying her gift of sight, but if she told the queen the truth, she might send her into a fit of despair.

"What was the second test?" Maeve asked, hoping its results might have been different.

"Ciara's preferred divining tool was scrying," Bradan said.

Maeve frowned. "What is that?"

"Fire gazing. I seldom use it myself, but Ciara had perfected the art of scrying. The flames had a way of drawing her into their depths and revealing a myriad of secrets.

"When Ciara returned to the castle the next day she asked the queen for a candle from the bedchamber the royal couple shared. A servant fetched it, the room was darkened and the candle lit. Ciara instructed the queen to stare at the flame and focus her thoughts on her husband and the child she hoped for. Then Ciara cleared her mind and gazed deep into the flame."

"What happened?" Maeve asked in a whisper.

"It was the same as before. The flame showed an empty cradle."

Maeve's heart twisted in her chest. "And Ciara had to tell the queen."

Bradan nodded. "She did not take it well. At first she didn't want to believe it. Then she lamented her failure as a wife. Her only duty was to give the king an heir, and she was unable to.

"To comfort her, Ciara told the queen the situation wasn't her fault. The dream and the flame had both revealed that the queen was as able as any woman to conceive and carry a child. It was the king who was wanting.

"Rather than placating her, the idea sent the queen into a rage. She accused Ciara of being a charlatan, then of lying and finally of having cast a spell on the queen so that she couldn't conceive."

"She had to know that was preposterous," Maeve said. "My mother had no reason to wish the queen ill—did she?"

Bradan shook his head. "No, but the queen was desperate. She couldn't blame the king, so she blamed Ciara. And the more she ranted, the more she came to believe her own words. Finally she pointed to Ciara's belly and shouted, 'A child for a child.' Ciara rushed from the castle, terrified of what might happen next."

Maeve was as upset as she knew Ciara must have been. "But she was only trying to help the queen."

It was as if Bradan hadn't heard her. "When Ciara returned to the Ruin and told me what had happened, she was sorely distressed. I wanted to think the queen's grief would pass and she would return to her senses, but Ciara had barely told me her tale when a child came running to say there were soldiers on the road with orders to arrest Ciara.

"Ciara was near her time. Fleeing would be too dangerous, so she went into hiding. For more than a week she kept herself in a little-known cave. Food and water were left for her, but otherwise no one went near her hiding place lest they give her away. We kept a lookout at a distance so help could be arranged when it was time for the babe to be born. In the meantime we were making plans to move Ciara and her child to safety.

"After a few days I began to hope the queen had given up. Word arrived that she and the king had returned to their castle in the north, taking their soldiers with them. Had I known the queen then as I do now, I would not have let my guard down. Queen Ailsa had not changed her mind—only her tactics. Instead of soldiers, she was employing spies.

"It took them only a few days to ferret out Ciara's hiding spot. When the lookout spotted the queen's agents, he whistled a warning to Ciara and bolted to the Ruin for help."

Bradan paused and Maeve could see it pained him to go on.

"I do not know the particulars of what happened after that. I can only assume that Ciara fled, for we found her a considerable distance from the cave. She was lying on the ground and bleeding badly from a blow to her head. But she was alive." Bradan's eyes brimmed with unshed tears. "Though her life was spent and she knew it, she fought for you to be born. She got to hold you only a few seconds, but before she died, she made me swear to keep you safe."

Chapter 14

The story weighed heavily on both the teller and the listener: Bradan mourned what had been lost while Maeve ached for that which had never been. Silence hung between them like wet wash.

It hadn't even been Ciara the queen was after. It was her unborn child—Maeve. In that respect, Ciara had bested the queen. She had seen Maeve born. And Bradan had kept Maeve safe, as he had promised—at least so far. The queen's piercing stare once more filled Maeve's mind, and she shook her head to chase it away.

"My head is too full," she said at last. "My heart as well. One spills over into the other, and I can't see sense in anything you've told me."

Bradan nodded. "I'm not sure there is any sense. You need time to think." Then he pulled himself up and shuffled down the path to the Ruin.

As Maeve watched him go, she felt her heart being squeezed. If only, she kept thinking. If only Bradan had been the one to counsel the queen. If only Ciara hadn't been so honest. If only the queen hadn't been inconsolable. And on it went—so many ifs. Had even one thing worked out differently, Ciara would still be alive.

And Maeve would have a mother. Anger and despair overwhelmed her. Her mother had been stolen from her. Encountering Ciara at the Bridge of Whispers made the situation even more bitter. Maeve could imagine Ciara in her life, and knowing that could never be was like a knife plunged into her heart.

When she saw the women gathering to begin the evening meal, she limped back to the Ruin. She had been wallowing in self-pity most of the afternoon. It was time to shake off her sullen mood.

Cara set her to work chopping greens. It was a tedious task but one she could do sitting down. Nearby Enda and Nora watched over the rabbits roasting on the fire.

"There needs be more heat," Enda declared, reaching for another log.

Nora slapped her hand away. "The heat is fine."

"No, it's not," her daughter argued. "Just look how low the fire is. There's barely any flame."

"You don't want a flame, daughter—unless you like your rabbit burned. What you want is steady heat."

Enda sent her mother an indignant glare. "This is not my first time cooking."

"You'd never know it," Nora snorted.

Maeve couldn't help smiling. Enda and Nora were always nattering, but there was no rancour in it. Bickering was simply their way of showing affection. Maeve felt a pang of melancholy as she wondered what sort of relationship she would have had with her mother.

"Tell me about her," Maeve said the next morning when she joined Bradan in the grove of oak trees. "I long to know what she was like."

Bradan looked puzzled. "I have already told you about Ciara."

"I don't mean the things anyone in the village can tell me. I want to know how she was with people who cared about her. What made her laugh—and cry? What made her angry? What did she want more than anything in the world?" Maeve threw up her arms. "I don't know, Bradan! But you do."

He heaved a resigned sigh. "Very well. I first met Ciara when she was twelve. I was—"

"Wait." Maeve put a hand on his arm. "You didn't meet Ciara until she was twelve? I thought you'd known her all her life. Was she not born here?"

"She was," Bradan said, "but I was not. I moved here to be her teacher."

"Where did you live before?"

Bradan raised an eyebrow. "I thought you wanted to learn about your mother."

"I do, but—"

"Then stop interrupting."

Maeve scowled and sat back. "Fine." She made a mental note to inquire about Bradan's early life at another time. Right now she wanted to find out about her mother, and she couldn't risk irritating him lest he change his mind about telling her.

"As I was saying"—he regarded her sternly—"I first met Ciara when she was twelve. She was precocious but in an endearing way. She was aware of how gifted she was but not obsessed with herself—nor overly impressed. She was glad to be a seer, but it didn't define her. She regarded her gift much as a fine whistler might value his skill at whistling.

"When I introduced myself, she said, 'You have a kind face. I think you will make a fine teacher.' Then she grinned and added, 'Perhaps we can teach each other.'"

Maeve gasped and covered her mouth. "Did she really say that?"

Bradan nodded. "She did."

"And what did you do?"

He spread his hands in resignation. "What could I do? She was merely expressing the facts as she perceived them. And I did learn from her. Not necessarily in the way she had implied, but ours was indeed a symbiotic relationship."

"What did she like to eat?" Maeve asked. There was so much she wanted to know.

"She didn't," Bradan said. "She was always too busy to eat and had to be reminded to do it."

"What made her laugh?"

"Everything. Her laughter was like the ringing of bells—a constant that cheered folk even if they didn't know the cause. She cried just as readily, for she was an empathetic soul. That was perhaps her most endearing quality. When folk spoke to her, she truly heard them, and that helped her be a better seer."

Maeve sighed. "She sounds wonderful."

"Indeed she had some wonderful qualities," Bradan agreed. "But she was not perfect. No one is."

"Oh." Maeve was genuinely surprised. "What was wrong with her?"

"She was wilful and exceedingly stubborn. Taken together, those qualities were sometimes a calamitous combination. On occasion it made her difficult to teach. She tended to resist ideas that disagreed with her own."

Maeve smiled and teased, "It's reassuring to know I'm not the only one to irritate you." And when Bradan raised an eyebrow again, she added wistfully, "I wish I had known her."

Bradan's face relaxed and he tapped his chest. "Even though you cannot be together in the usual way, the bond between you is strong. Why do you think you see her at the Bridge of Whispers? Her mother's love feels your need."

Once again Bradan cut Maeve's lesson short, and she was glad of it for she couldn't concentrate. As soon as Bradan let her go, she hurried to the Bridge of Whispers. Her ankle was much improved. Though she took her stick with her, she had no need of it—unless the queen's woman made another attempt on her life.

To her great relief, Ciara was at the stream when she arrived. She was standing on the bridge, gazing into the water, exactly as she had been the first time Maeve had seen her. She must have sensed Maeve's presence, for she turned and smiled.

Maeve returned her smiled and waved, then watched as Ciara moved to the grass on the verge of the forest. She beckoned Maeve to join her.

Maeve picked her way over the rocks until she was so near Ciara she could have touched her. At least she could have if her mother were alive. But Maeve suspected her hand would pass straight through her, just as it had done with Ciara's fire.

As if her thoughts had conjured it, a fire appeared on the ground between them. Maeve caught her breath. She knew the fire was her mother's doing, but the timing was uncanny. For a moment she watched the flames flicker and then she glanced up at Ciara.

"You have something to show me?"

Ciara turned her attention back to the fire, so Maeve did the same. Having looked into the flames before, she knew to relax her gaze so that her vision blurred. After a few seconds it cleared again, and there was Queen Ailsa, just as she'd been at the council of war and in Maeve's memory ever since.

Maeve sent Ciara a puzzled look. "Mother, I know the queen was your enemy and that she is mine as well. I know I am in danger. You have already shown me that."

Ciara gestured to the fire.

Maeve turned to look, and the queen's piercing stare immediately filled her mind. But even as she watched, the face began to melt, its features distorted beyond recognition. Maeve shuddered to see the queen's beauty stretch and twist until it transformed into a totally different image. It was still the queen, but now she was running across a scrubby field toward a woodland. As she entered the trees, she turned to look back at a castle. And then the fire vanished.

Maeve blinked, hoping she'd only imagined the fire had disappeared. She needed to see more.

Maeve looked to her mother, but Ciara was gone too. Maeve knew there was no point wishing her back.

Ciara's fire had shown the queen running from a castle toward the woods. Was it possible she had escaped?

Chapter 15

As Maeve hurried back to the Ruin, she imagined the queen's thugs lurking behind every tree and bush. She'd known for several days that she was in danger, but the two attempts on her life were too much like accidents—as if they were meant only to scare her. But if the queen were free, Maeve was well and truly afraid.

In the queen's mind, Ciara had cast a spell, causing her to be childless. And she had sworn revenge. A child for a child. Maeve was that child. The queen had been tricked into believing Maeve was dead, which likely fueled her anger. Then Maeve's interpretation of King Redmond's dream had led to the queen's imprisonment. If the queen had wanted revenge before, she would be even more bent on it now.

Considering all the queen had done, she couldn't be in her right mind. And that made her all the more dangerous. The woman was powerful and set on revenge. And she'd killed before.

For the remainder of the day, Maeve stayed near the Ruin, but even as she attended to her chores, she kept one eye on the forest.

That night she went to bed knowing she wouldn't sleep. It wasn't fear keeping her awake so much as a feeling that something wasn't right. And if she had learned anything during her brief training as a seer, it was to trust her instincts.

Not wanting to disturb Enda, she lay very still as she tried to make sense of the situation. The more she thought about it, the more convinced she was that the queen had escaped. The question was what was she planning to do next.

The quartz at Maeve's neck began to throb with warmth. She placed her hand over it and slid out from under the coverlet. Then quietly padding to the door, she tugged on her boots, wrapped herself in her mantle and let herself out of the sleeping chamber and into the night.

Behind her the Ruin continued to sleep. Above, the stars winked from a cloudless sky. The remnants of the cooking fire cast a dim light. Maeve made her way to it, poked the remaining char with a stick until the embers glowed, and then dropped on some kindling and a small log. The new wood crackled and snapped the dying fire back to life. The flame didn't provide a great deal of light, but it would be enough for Maeve's purposes.

As she reached for the quartz and began to lift it over her head, the heat left the stone. Her pendulum had never done that before. It had become warm while she was in bed thinking, an indication that it had something to tell her, but now that she was preparing to speak with it, it had grown cold.

It was odd, but Maeve couldn't worry about that now. She needed a question answered. In one fluid movement she removed the pendulum and held it in her hand as she got in position to begin.

"Ow!" She released the stone and snatched up the chain with her other hand before it could drop to the ground. The quartz was so cold it had burned her. She held her hand to the light of the fire. There was a mark where the stone had been.

Dangling it by its chain, Maeve studied the quartz. It didn't look any different. "What are you trying to tell me?" she said in a whisper. Cautiously she placed a finger on one of its facets. It was neither warm nor cold. She lowered the pendulum into her hand again. It felt as it always did. She shook her head. This was very strange. "Won't you answer my questions?" she asked it.

The quartz became pleasantly warm once more, and Maeve relaxed.

"Thank you," she said. "Let us begin then." But she had no sooner uttered the words than the stone turned cold once more—not so cold that it burned her, but enough to make her hesitate. She stared down at it. In the firelight it glinted all the colours of a rainbow. "I don't understand." She frowned. "What are you trying to tell me? You want to speak to me, but as soon as I try to let you, you stop me."

The stone became warm once more. It had a mind of its own this night. It wanted to communicate, but at the same time, it didn't. Was this the moodiness of pendulums Bradan had warned her about? Her pendulum had never done this before. Of course, she had never tried to speak with it in the middle of the night either. Perhaps it was tired. Did pendulums get tired?

The quartz became cool. Maeve took that to be a no. She frowned. If that wasn't the problem, what was? All the times she'd spoken to her pendulum at the Bridge of Whispers, it had been most cooperative.

The stone became warm once more. Was that it? Did it want her to go to the bridge? Would it answer her questions there? The pendulum became even warmer.

Maeve looked toward the forest. She couldn't see it, but she could feel it. She frowned. Her enemies could be lying in wait there. Her pendulum was telling her to go. Should she listen to her head or trust her instinct? Bradan was always urging her to think. But he also said she should have faith in what her heart told her.

Finally Maeve slipped the chain over her head and tucked the quartz inside her robe. She looked back at the Ruin and then into the night hiding the forest. Grabbing a torch from the nearby rack, she stuck the head of it into the fire. As the pitch caught and hissed and then burst into flame, the quartz at her throat pulsed its approval.

Maeve moved slowly toward the forest, holding the torch high. She looked anxiously from side to side, ready to turn and run should needs be. But once she stepped into the trees, the forest welcomed her as it always did and her anxiety left her.

Buoyed by relief and a need to reach the bridge, Maeve hurried on. The torchlight threw shadows onto the trees so that they no longer seemed familiar. But even in the unnerving darkness, her feet knew the way. She heard the stream before she saw it, and when she reached its rocky bank, she trod carefully until she was at the bridge.

Allowing herself a deep, calming breath, she drove the base of the torch into the dirt at the foot of the bridge and freed the pendulum from her neck. This time it didn't protest.

Maeve had to hurry. The longer she was away from the Ruin the more likely her absence would be noticed. She readied herself and her pendulum and began.

"Pendulum." She wasn't speaking loudly, but even so her voice was like thunder splitting the silence of the night. "Need I be fearful the queen has escaped?"

She held her breath, waiting for the pendulum to move. It couldn't have been more than a few seconds but it felt like an eternity. Finally the crystal began to circle.

Yes.

Maeve gulped and her hand jerked involuntarily, pulling the quartz from its arc. She steadied her arm and took several deep breaths to calm herself.

"Pendulum, is the queen coming after me?"

The chain shifted between her fingers as if to swing the quartz in a yes circle again, but then it stopped. Maeve stared hard at her hand. Had she accidentally caused it to move? As she pondered the possibility, the chain shifted again and began to carve out a circle in the other direction. No. Her pendulum was telling her no! The queen wasn't chasing her.

Maeve's first reaction was relief, but it was short-lived. The pendulum's answer didn't make sense. She hadn't imagined the two attempts on her life.

She steadied the pendulum once more and said, "Pendulum, did the queen try to have me killed?"

Yes.

Maeve frowned. The pendulum's answers seemed to contradict one another. Perhaps she needed to be more specific. She thought for a moment and then said, "Pendulum, does the queen want me dead right now?"

Again the answer came quickly.

No.

Maeve didn't know what to think. She thanked her pendulum, dropped her arm and slid down the wall of the bridge.

The queen had wanted her dead, but now she didn't. Why? Something had changed, but what? She wouldn't have given up. She was up to something.

As Maeve tried to make sense of the situation, she leaned her head against the stone and gazed at the torch. The ball of flame billowed and swayed while fiery tongues licked the darkness, pulling in the night—and Maeve.

Her eyelids grew heavy and the fire became a blur. She told herself she should get back to the Ruin, but she didn't want to move. It was as if her spirit was dancing with the flame, the two twined as one. She let her thoughts wander deep into the fire.

And there was Deirdre. She looked happy. She was cradling her belly, blissfully imagining the child she would soon hold in her arms. Maeve could see it on her face. It buoyed her spirits to think she would be with her sister to share that time.

Then a snap and pop startled Maeve from her reverie, and though she continued to stare into the fire, Deirdre was gone. Now there was naught but flame. The pitch popped again and whispered, "A child for a child."

Chapter 16

Maeve's body jerked and she banged her head on the stone wall of the bridge, but she barely noticed. She was too horrified by what she'd heard.

A child for a child. She knew exactly what the words meant. Queen Ailsa had changed targets. It was no longer Maeve she was after—it was Deirdre's child.

She scrambled to her feet and grabbed the torch. She had to get back to the Ruin and tell Bradan. They had to stop the queen before it was too late.

She was only a few steps into the forest when what sounded like an animal moving through the undergrowth made her freeze. She held her breath and listened. Everything in the forest was asleep as it should be. She must have imagined the noise. She was about to resume walking when she heard the rustling again. She peered into the night—as if that would somehow help her hear better.

And then it came a third time—bushes moving and twigs snapping. Maeve tried to determine where the noise was coming from. In the dark forest, sound had a way of bouncing off trees and playing tricks with one's mind. The rustling could be coming from anywhere. But it was getting louder.

Maeve had been sure the forest was hiding no enemies, but what if she'd been wrong? She glanced up at the torch she was carrying. If someone was hunting her, the flame gave away her location. She dropped the torch to the ground and smothered the flame with dirt.

In an instant the night turned to pitch. Maeve couldn't see anything, but she had to get moving. If one of the queen's henchmen was after her, he need only hurry toward the memory of the torchlight.

Which way should she go? Fear had disoriented her. She told herself to remain calm. Panicking would only make the situation worse. She closed her eyes and tried to picture the forest as it had looked in the torchlight. When she could visualize the path in her mind, she moved forward as quickly as she dared.

The rustling and snapping started up again. Maeve picked up her pace. The sound was getting closer. Or was she only imagining that?

Suddenly it stopped. Maeve stopped. She listened. Nothing.

For a good minute she stood as still as a statue, straining to pick out any sound at all. Though the night remained silent, she had a bad feeling.

She had to get back to the Ruin. She began to run. No longer sure where the path was, she crashed through the undergrowth, scratching her face on leafless branches and stumbling over exposed tree roots. She paused to catch her breath and get her bearings. For all she knew, she was headed back the way she'd come.

She might not be able to see, but she still had her other senses, so she focused on them. She picked up the faint scent of freshly chopped wood—the woodpile at the edge of the forest. She turned herself toward it. Then she slid her foot from side to side along the ground, searching for the trail. She reached out her arms to locate the bushes, ferns and trees flanking the path. Satisfied at last that she knew where she was and where she was going, she again started to run.

And slammed straight into something—no, someone. She was immediately caught up in a fierce hug that pinned her arms to her sides. Before she could scream, a hand covered her mouth.

Maeve was terrified. Finding the fleshy part of a finger pressing on her teeth, she clamped down on it as hard as she could.

It had the desired effect. Her attacker bellowed in pain and let her go.

"Aaagghh! By Taliesin's beard, Maeve! You almost bit my finger off!"

Poised to flee, Maeve spun around. "Declan?"

"Of course Declan!"

"I'm so sorry," she said. "I truly am. I would never have bitten so hard if I'd known it was you."

"But you still would have bitten me?"

"You know what I mean. What are you doing out here in the middle of the night?"

"I might ask the same of you."

"I asked first," Maeve shot back stubbornly.

"I was worried about you," Declan replied. "Something is going on. In a matter of days you've had two accidents that could have had grave consequences. And you've been secretive and preoccupied." He reached for Maeve's hands and squeezed them. "I couldn't sleep, so I stepped outside to get some night air. I saw you leave the Ruin. When you headed into the forest I followed you.

"Your turn. Why did you go to the forest in the middle of the night?"

"My pendulum pressed me to go. It needed me to ask it a question."

"How could a pendulum need you to ask a question? That makes no sense."

"Well it did," said Maeve.

"All right," said Declan. "Did you find out what it wanted you to know?"

"I did," she said. "And a good thing too, because it's a matter of life and death."

His grip on her hands tightened. "Yours?"

Maeve could hear the concern in his voice. "No," she replied. "At least not at the moment. Let's get back to the Ruin and I'll explain."

The next morning Maeve stopped Bradan as he made his way to his breakfast.

"I must tell you something," she said.

"What is it?" He frowned.

"The queen has escaped."

Bradan pulled back. "When? How do you know this?"

Maeve shook her head. "Recently I think. Ciara showed me in a fire yesterday."

The old Druid's eyebrows jumped up. "You didn't tell me."

"I needed to be sure. So last night I went back to the Bridge of Whispers and asked my pendulum."

"That was foolish," Bradan scolded her. "There have already been two attempts on your life. You have to assume your enemies are watching your every move. Alone in the forest at night, you were an easy target."

Maeve hung her head. "I'm sorry, but I felt I must."

"Why could it not have waited until morning? And why did you have to go to the bridge?"

"My pendulum was urging me. You said yourself I must follow my instincts. That's what I was doing. I was certain my pendulum wanted me to go to the bridge, so I went. I was using my gift."

The old man opened his mouth and then closed it again. After a moment he said, "Continue."

So Maeve explained what had happened. She

told him what she'd seen and heard in the flames. As she was speaking, Declan joined them.

"What I don't understand is how Queen Ailsa knows about Deirdre," Declan said when she had finished.

"That is a good point," Bradan agreed. "How does she know of Deirdre and her condition? Even if the queen has eyes on you, Deirdre has not been to the Ruin, nor have you been back to your village. The queen knows naught of your life there."

The three fell silent.

"Unless—" Maeve muttered.

"Unless what?" Bradan and Declan asked in unison.

She looked up. "Unless that woman, Una, knew. She is the queen's servant. And Enda told her a great deal about me. Perhaps she mentioned Deirdre. I shall ask her before Declan and I leave."

"Leave?" Bradan frowned. "Where are you going?"

"To warn Deirdre."

"You can't," Bradan protested. "You'll be risking your own life. The queen won't hesitate to kill you if you cross her path. You'll be safer here at the Ruin."

Maeve shook her head. "It is because of me that Deirdre and her child are in danger. I am going. I must."

"I'm sorry," Enda said as Maeve scurried about the sleeping chamber, stuffing things into her pack. "I didn't know. I thought it was harmless small talk is all."

"Clearly it wasn't," said Maeve as she glared at her friend. Then noting Enda's downcast expression, she softened and added, "But it can't be helped now. Did you tell Una where Deirdre lives?"

"No." Enda shook her head. "I didn't. I couldn't. I don't know, do I?"

That was something to be thankful for, Maeve supposed. It wouldn't take long for the queen's henchmen to ferret out that information, though—an innocent inquiry in the village would do it. There were always tongues eager to wag. Enda wasn't alone in that. Still, it would slow Deirdre's pursuers. Maeve hoped it would be enough.

Declan and Bradan were waiting for her at the stone bench in front of the Ruin.

"Stay to the backroads," Bradan said. "Try not to be seen. There is no way to tell who is spying for the queen."

"We will," Declan promised.

Maeve nodded. "I can't say how long we'll be gone."

Bradan put a hand on her arm. "Take care—both of you—and come back safely."

Maeve hugged him. "We will. Try not to worry."

Chapter 17

Maeve and Declan were young and fleet of foot, and though they kept to the rougher terrain, they quickly put the miles behind them. Even so, Maeve couldn't shake the feeling that they were being watched. They overnighted in a wood and arrived in the Eastern Kingdom by noon the following day. The farm where Deirdre lived with her husband and his family lay south of the village, which meant the two young people could go directly there without attracting unwanted attention.

"Will she come away with you?" Declan asked as they huddled in the trees on the edge of the wood, watching the cottage and outbuildings for signs of the queen's henchmen. There were no people about. Just a few sheep and cows grazing in a field and a horse straining to reach a pile of hay in the back of a cart.

"She has to," Maeve replied. "She isn't safe here."

"You know that," Declan said, "but can you convince her? You're asking her to believe a far-fetched tale. She might well think you've lost your mind."

Maeve shot him a withering glare. "My mind is perfectly fine."

"I know that, but your sister doesn't."

"She will once I've explained everything. Then we'll hide her in Riasc Tiarna's cave. It's nearby. The queen's minions won't find her there, and I'm sure the dragon lord won't mind us using it. When the immediate danger has passed, we can find a place more suitable." She scanned the area one more time and stepped out from the trees. "Come. We must hurry."

Maeve and Declan bounded across the clearing to the cottage door. Their knock was answered by Deirdre's mother-in-law, whose eyes narrowed suspiciously the second she saw them.

"Good day, mistress." Maeve smiled, hoping to put the woman at ease. "Do you remember me? I'm Deirdre's sister, Maeve."

The woman studied her a moment longer and then her face relaxed and she nodded. "What are you doing here? I heard tell you're with the Druids now."

"Yes," Maeve nodded. "That is true, but Deirdre asked me to be with her when her baby is born. And since a body can't know exactly when it will be her time, I've come now." She gestured to Declan. "This is my friend. He accompanied me on the road."

The woman didn't even look at Declan. "She's not here," she said abruptly. "Left for the village market yesterday morning and she's not returned."

Maeve felt her body grow weak as if the blood was draining from her. She tried to keep the alarm from her voice as she asked, "Might she have stayed with a friend?"

The woman shook her head. "I can't see why—unless the child decided to come early. But then someone would ha' told us, you'd think." She shrugged. "Even so, that's the only thing what makes sense. She'd not run off, bein' with child and all. And besides, she'd no call to leave. Fergus treats her well and I have no quarrel with her."

"I shall go to the village and make inquiries," Maeve said.

"That's what Fergus is doing now," the woman replied. "If you find her, put her on the road home." Then she shut the door.

Maeve turned to Declan. "I fear we are too late."

"Don't be quick to judgment." He placed his hands on her shoulders. "There may be a reasonable explanation for her absence. We shall go to the village and make inquiries."

Maeve nodded and bolted for the road. She wanted to believe Declan was right, but the twisting in her stomach said otherwise.

The dirt track, wide enough for only a cart, cut through farmland, then disappeared into the forest and came out again at the village. Maeve scoured the knee-high grass to the right of the track while Declan did the same on the left. They reasoned that since Fergus was already searching for Deirdre, he would have followed the road, and if there was anything that had escaped his notice, it would be found on the verges. Maeve hoped they would discover nothing and that Deirdre had merely stayed over in the village. But she was doubtful.

"I've seen nothing suspicious," Declan said when they reached the edge of the forest.

"Nor have I," she called back. "That's good, I suppose, but we have to keep looking."

About ten steps into the trees, Maeve spied hoofprints in the damp ground. They led away from the road. She followed them to a tiny clearing. The ground was badly gouged as if a horse had been stamping in place. There were bootprints as well—one large set and another much smaller.

As Maeve studied the area, something else caught her eye. She hurried to where a basket lay overturned beside a bush. She righted it, but there was nothing inside.

Then her heart began to pound so hard it boomed in her ears. She recognized the workmanship. All the reeds were dark except for a single band of light ones running through the middle. Deirdre had made this. Maeve had seen her sister weave hundreds of baskets. The light band was her signature.

"Declan!" she shouted. "I've found Deirdre's basket. Come quickly!"

When she received no reply she spun around to call again, but a scream jumped into her throat instead. On the other side of the road she watched Declan crumple to the ground at the feet of a man with a cudgel. The man raised his head, looked directly at her and leered.

"No!" she cried. She would have run at him, save for a loud crack followed by a sharp pain in her head—and then nothing.

Maeve awoke to woolly darkness and a terrible throbbing in her head. She was lying on her side and something hard was pressing into her cheek. She tried to turn away from it, but the small movement sent a jagged pain ripping through her brain. Nausea rose in her gorge, and she noticed she was gagged. The wadded cloth stuffed into her mouth was wet with her spit and made it hard for her to swallow. She pulled against the scratchy rope that bound her hands behind her and realized it was knotted around her neck as well. She tried to straighten her legs but the same rope bound her ankles, causing the part around her neck to tighten and chafe her skin. She'd been bound so that any movement at all would choke her.

She tried to scream but could not. Again she tried to move her head. Again the pain seared her brain. Tears sprang to her eyes. Where was she? Where was Declan? It suddenly struck Maeve that she was completely alone, and that realization sucked away the last of her hope. *Help me!* she silently pleaded as she wept. *Someone please help me.*

She felt the crystal beneath her robe begin to pulse. The stone's familiar warmth couldn't free her from the rope binding her, but it distracted her and stemmed her weeping. And as her panic ebbed, she noticed the silver ring on her hand had shifted. It had turned on her thumb. She hadn't moved it. It had turned itself. The ring and the crystal were trying to speak to her.

Ciara was with her. And another spirit as well it would seem. She wasn't alone.

That thought buoyed her spirits. She had many more friends than enemies, and those friends would find her. She need only survive until they did. She was a seer. She was young and strong, and she was resourceful. She would find a way out of this. Her mind settled and she started to think.

She wasn't in immediate danger. Otherwise she would be dead already.

She opened her senses to her surroundings. She couldn't have been unconscious for long, so she wasn't far from where she and Declan had been searching. She felt her heart twist. She'd seen Declan go down. Where was he now? Was he all right?

The not knowing made her heart ache, so Maeve forced herself to concentrate on her own situation. It must be early afternoon—and yet it was dark. She was lying on a hard surface beneath a heavy covering. From the smell of it, she guessed it was a woollen blanket. And she was being jostled. She was moving—probably in a cart. She could hear the jangle of harness and the clop of hooves.

They must be heading north, for the road south went no further than Deirdre's home. They had to be going toward the village. There would be people there. If she could figure out a way to make her predicament known, she might find help.

For a time she stayed still and planned her escape. She conjured an image of the village in her mind. The road ran through the centre of the market before leading out the other side. If she could draw attention to herself, she might be rescued. She was going to have to roll out from under the blanket so someone would see her. But she needed to do it in such a way that she didn't strangle herself.

When she heard the first buzz of voices—the familiar sound of vendors peddling their wares—she felt behind her for the blanket. It was right there, yet it eluded her grasp. For several minutes she struggled to grab hold of it. Finally she caught the edge. This small victory lifted her spirits. When she rolled she would take the cover with her, and the villagers would see she was being held prisoner.

The voices were getting louder. Her opportunity was only a moment away. Pulling her legs and arms upward behind her, she made the rope as slack as possible and readied herself to roll.

Something hard dug into her back and a gruff male voice near her ear said, "Move and you die."

As the sounds of the village faded, tears rolled down Maeve's cheeks. Never had she been so without hope. Her head was throbbing and her body ached. Even breathing was difficult.

She tried to stretch her legs for some relief, but the rope around her neck immediately grew taut, chafing and burning her already raw skin. She quickly drew her legs back up. She didn't know how much more she could bear. Perhaps she should have let herself be killed in the village. At least her torture would be over.

They don't want you dead. The thought came from nowhere but instantly took up all the space in Maeve's head. *The queen wants you alive.*

Maeve knew what she must do. Without a second's thought, she began straining against her fetters and rolling on the bed of the cart, heedless of the physical distress it caused. The blanket slid away, and she could once more see daylight.

She saw her abductors standing in the front of the cart. Her struggling had drawn their attention and the driver was pulling on the reins to slow the horse. The other man dropped onto Maeve to still her thrashing.

"Mallacht na baintrí ort! A widow's curse upon you, girl!" he growled. "Why must you make things difficult?"

Maeve was sure she was going to choke to death or gag on her own spit. She couldn't cough for the rag in her mouth, and she couldn't breathe. Panic set her thrashing once more.

"If you want to live, be still!" the man shouted as he pulled a large knife from a sheath hanging on his belt.

But Maeve couldn't have stopped writhing if she'd wanted to. Her panic to be free was greater than her fear of death. Kill me, she thought. A blade across her throat or through her heart couldn't be worse than this slow strangulation.

With one swift motion the knife swooped toward her. There was a sharp tug and then a release. Maeve wondered if she was dead.

Chapter 18

The rope was no longer pressing on her throat. Her abductor ripped the gag from her mouth, allowing blessed air to rush into her lungs. Maeve gulped it in and coughed until her throat was raw.

The man cut the length of rope joining her hands and ankles and roughly yanked her to a sitting position. The relief was so intense Maeve wondered why she didn't float away. Her hands and ankles were still bound, but she was able to stretch her legs for the first time in hours.

"Drink." The driver held a waterskin to her lips. She gulped the liquid and was immediately taken by another bout of coughing. The water poured down her chin and robe, but she barely noticed. The man who'd offered her water was the one who had stood over Declan with a cudgel.

When her heart had finally stopped racing and she could breathe without coughing, she said, "Who are you and what do you want with me? What have you done with my friend?"

"You ask too many questions," he growled. "Unless you wish to be bound again, you will hold your tongue."

It was as if Maeve hadn't heard. "Where are you taking me? Are you the queen's servants?"

The man stuffed the gag back into her mouth and produced another length of rope. Maeve felt her panic surge once more. The thought of being bound again was terrifying. Her captor dragged her by the arm to the middle of the cart near the inner wall and lashed her hands to one of the staves, though thankfully he did not again truss her like a pheasant. When he dropped a sack over her head, the darkness returned. As the two men climbed aboard, she felt the cart shift, and then it jerked forward.

It was twilight when they finally stopped for the night and one of the men removed the sack. She tried to think where they could be. Though the light was dim, she could see they were in a small grove amid rolling hills. She looked up. There were no stars or moon to help her with direction. Maeve hadn't sensed any turns during the journey, so they were probably still heading north. She inhaled the night air. It was heavy with earthy smells, but there was a hint of the sea as well. They were probably following the coastline.

But where were they taking her?

One of the men removed the rope binding her to the cart and untied her hands and feet. Then he unknotted the noose around her neck.

Free! She was free! It felt so good.

For a brief moment.

And then, to Maeve's horror, the man took the rope he'd used to lash her to the cart and—trapping her against the staves with his knee—tied a new noose around her neck. She tried to break away, screaming and pounding him with her fists, but he was too big and too strong to be affected.

"Enough!" he bellowed, jumping down from the cart. He gave the rope a tug so fierce it yanked Maeve the length of the cart and off the back. She fell to the ground in a coughing heap. "Get up," he ordered and began walking deeper into the trees.

Eventually he stopped and tied the free end of the rope high on the trunk of a tree. Besides being fearful, Maeve felt humiliated. She was tethered like an animal. Even at the house of Eamon the blacksmith she'd never been treated this cruelly.

"Do your business," the man said, "and be quick about it. I will be back. Do not try to escape, for I will hunt you down and kill you."

As Maeve watched him stride away, she had no doubt he meant what he'd said. She peered into the growing gloom. Even if she could untie the rope, there was nowhere to hide. All she could do was try to stay calm, keep her wits about her and do her best to survive. *They don't want me dead*, she reminded herself and tried desperately to believe it.

Maeve and her abductors were on the road for three days and two nights. She quickly learned that if she didn't speak and didn't struggle, life was tolerable. She was fed and watered but otherwise ignored. She was bound in one way or another at all times—even when she slept—and the sack was placed over her head while they were on the move.

The men didn't want her to know where she was being taken. But Bradan's relentless lessons had not gone to waste. Maeve's senses were acute, as were her powers of deduction. When they were about midway up the coast, they turned inland. She could tell by the feel and smell of the air and also by the horse's laboured gait. The cart wheels turned slower and bumped more. The terrain was steeper and more rugged. They were heading into Meath.

On the third day they stopped well before dark. Maeve remained in the cart—bound and hooded—while her captors sat at a distance, talking. They kept their voices low, and Maeve couldn't make out what they were saying. She had a feeling her journey with them had come to an end. They were waiting for something.

It wasn't until darkness fell that she sensed the presence of someone else. The men stopped talking. Then there was scuffling as they got to their feet and batted the dust from their breeches.

"You have the girl?" a woman asked. Maeve knew the voice.

"You have our silver?" It was one of her captors. There was a metallic jingle. A purse being exchanged, Maeve guessed.

"Fetch her," the woman said.

She heard the crunch of boots on the dirt road and then felt the rope being tied around her neck. She knew better than to struggle. When her hands were freed, the man tugged on the rope. "Come."

"I can't see where I'm going. Can you remove the sack?"

"That is for someone else. My friend and I are done with you." But instead of leading her by her tether as she had expected, he gripped her arm and pulled her along beside him.

Moving quickly and blindly, Maeve stumbled, but the man's firm hold ensured she did not fall.

"She is unharmed as you can see," he said when they reached the others.

"How do I know you have brought me the right girl?" the woman asked. "Remove the hood."

"Are you not concerned she will remember your face and this place?" one of the men asked.

The woman laughed without amusement. "It is of no concern. She won't have occasion to tell anyone. Remove the hood."

It was a relief to leave the stifling darkness of the sack for the dusty shadows of twilight.

"Hello, Una," she said. She refused to show her fear. "Enda and I were wondering where you'd gotten to."

Una smirked.

"If you're satisfied with the goods, we'll take our leave," one of the men said. "But I'd keep a sharp eye on this one. She's wily."

After the men turned the cart around and headed off the way they'd come, Maeve became aware of another person lurking in the shadows.

"Ion!" Una called sharply, and a chubby young man came running. It was not a warm evening, but he was sweating profusely, and the smell of him caused Maeve to fall back a step.

"Yes, Ma. I-I-I mean, yes, my lady," he stuttered.

So Una had a son.

Maeve couldn't see the expression on Una's face, but her exasperated growl left no doubt about her disgust.

She held out the end of the rope to the lad and said, "Lead our guest to her lodgings." When Ion didn't immediately move, she barked, "Go!"

Even in the deepening darkness without a torch, Ion seemed to know his way, and Maeve had only to follow the rasp of his wheezing and the tug of the rope. She gripped it in her hands to keep it from pulling on her neck. As she stumbled along behind, she assessed her situation.

She was now the queen's prisoner. But what did Queen Ailsa have planned for her? And where was she? Where was Declan? And Deirdre? Was her sister safe? Maeve had so many questions, but she would not ask Una a single one. It would tell the woman how much information Maeve had, and she would use that knowledge to her advantage. Maeve needed to minimize Una's power—not add to it.

She looked up into the sky. The stars were splashed across the entire night, and climbing into their midst was the milk-white, almost-ripe moon. It pushed itself up from a rocky hill and paused for a moment behind a black silhouette looming above them. It was a dark fortress. Maeve smiled to herself. Castle Carrick. She should have guessed.

It was as if the moon and stars had been placed in the sky for the sole purpose of revealing the castle to Maeve, and now that she had seen it, clouds rolled in to take over the night. She expected Ion to head for the steep road that led to the main gates, but instead he took them behind the fortress into a woodland. After a time he stopped beside a large outcropping of rock.

It had begun to rain and the wind had come up. Maeve wondered how much longer it would be before they reached the queen—for she was sure that was where she was being taken. She glanced back at the castle and once again found herself gazing into Ciara's fire at the Bridge of Whispers, watching the queen run from a castle. At the time she had assumed it was the castle in which the queen had been imprisoned, but it occurred to Maeve now that perhaps it was not.

A raindrop fell on her nose and another onto her cheek. She pulled up the hood of her mantle.

Una pushed past her and grabbed the end of the tether from Ion. "Get on with it," she snapped.

"Yes, lady," he grovelled, turning toward the small mountain of rock. A log lay on the ground in front, and after much puffing and grunting he managed to roll it away. Then he ran his hand along the surface of the outcropping, searching for something. Finally his fingers closed around a rock wedged between two larger ones. He pushed on it until it slid deep into the crevice.

A grating sound and a tremble in the ground beneath Maeve's feet caused her to jump back. Then, to her amazement, one of the large rocks began to move away from the rest, as though it were a door opening on a hinge.

When the boulder had fully pulled away from the rest of the rock formation, Maeve blinked in disbelief. Before her was a narrow stairway leading down. Torches hung on the walls inside the entrance. Impatiently shoving the end of Maeve's tether into Ion's hand, Una snatched one up and started down the stairs. Shortening Maeve's lead, Ion followed, pulling Maeve after him. Once they were inside, he pressed another stone and the boulder scraped shut.

A light breeze blew through the stairwell and the torchlight flickered. Holding fast to the rope around her neck with one hand, Maeve placed the other on the wall to steady herself.

When they reached the bottom, they continued along a dark tunnel that sloped upward. It twisted and turned but eventually levelled out and gave way to a hallway sparsely lit by torches and marked by a series of heavy wooden doors, each with a barred opening near the top. Maeve decided they must be in the belly of the castle and this must be the dungeon. It smelled dank. Water dripped from the ceiling and trickled down the rough stone walls. Maeve shivered and prayed to Brighid that this would not be her new home.

As they walked on, the smell became stronger, and when they turned a corner, Maeve saw a great pool of stagnant water laced with green and brown algae. She peered into its depths, wondering what lurked beneath the surface. The pool was walled on three sides, and jutting from two of them was a progression of roughly hewn stones—a stairway of sorts. As Una moved toward them, Maeve realized she was going to have to climb them. She shuddered at the thought of misstepping and falling into the pool. Ion must have felt her pull back on her tether, for he turned to her and scowled. "Do not resist and do not fall. It will not go well for either of us."

Maeve couldn't imagine things would go well for her in any case, but she swallowed her fear and climbed the stairs with care. She was relieved to reach the top and step into another hallway. This one was wider and better lit than the last, and the doors running its length had no peepholes. Servants' quarters, she decided. Beside one door sat a stool and a small table. It struck her as odd, since there were no other such furnishings anywhere else in the hall. As they moved quickly past, she thought she detected a flickering light under the door. Were there servants in the castle even with King Owen gone? Or was this Ion's chamber?

The hallway continued some distance before opening onto a room flanked by two circular towers of stairs that wound their way to the top of the castle. Maeve remembered them from her time here during the council of war, except then they had been well lit. Now they were in darkness. But Una had her torch, and without pausing she led them up to the main foyer and into the Great Hall.

Maeve was shocked to see the change. When last she'd been here this room had vibrated with life. It had been grand and opulent, but now it was bleak. The first thing she noticed was the fire. Instead of the mighty blaze she remembered, this fire was puny, casting little heat or light. In the shadows beyond it, Maeve could make out a grand chair—a throne—and someone sitting on it. It could only be the queen.

A jagged white dagger of lightning ripped the sky and flooded the Great Hall with light. Then the darkness returned, accompanied by a murderous clap of thunder.

"Welcome, dear," Queen Ailsa said. "Maeve, is it not?"

Maeve straightened her shoulders and lifted her chin. "You know well it is."

The queen's voice hardened. "Yes."

The quartz around Maeve's throat pulsed and quelled the anger growing in her. "I am surprised to see you at Castle Carrick, Lady," she remarked. "I would have thought this would be the first place King Redmond would search for you."

The queen shook her head. "When he imprisoned my brother, he relieved him of his title and lands. Since then the castle has been locked tight, awaiting a new king of Meath. A cockroach would be hard-pressed to find a way in."

"And yet you have managed it," Maeve said.

The queen didn't notice or didn't acknowledge the insult. "One of the advantages of having grown up here. I know of the hidden entry. My husband, the king, does not."

"You did not take measures to hide it from me."

"You won't be telling anyone." She swept her arm through the air. "Enough of this talk. I prefer to discuss the reason I have brought you here. The time has come to even the score."

"There is no score to even," Maeve replied. "I know of your grievance with my mother and it is without cause. You are childless through no fault of your own nor of my mother. It is only your pain that drives you."

"Silence!" the queen ordered her. "You know nothing."

"I know that you were hurt and you took your pain out on my mother. You needed someone to lash out at and you chose her. She tried to help you, but because she was with child and you were not—and could never be—you let your hurt turn to hate."

"She cursed me!" the queen growled.

"You know that is untrue," Maeve replied evenly. "She had no cause."

"She did!" Queen Ailsa shouted.

Maeve shook her head. "She did not. Her mistake was in telling you the truth. The king could not give you a child."

"That is a lie!" the queen shouted.

Maeve shrugged. "I cannot convince you any more than my mother could. But that changes nothing."

"A child for a child." The queen's eyes narrowed with rancour. "It is what I've sworn and it is what I will have."

"So kill me and be done."

The queen laughed; it was an ugly sound. "Oh, I shall—have no fear—but there is more to it now. Your mother took my child and I shall take hers. It is fair payment. But over the years much has happened and the stakes have grown. I have been cheated of my revenge for too long because of the interference of that meddling old Druid and that troublesome dragon. Your death alone is no longer enough."

What did Riasc Tiarna have to do with all of this, Maeve wondered. But she had no time to puzzle over the matter for the queen was still speaking.

"You have proven to be as aggravating a creature as your mother. If not for your interference, my brother would be ruling this land—as he should have been all along. Now Owen languishes in a dungeon and Redmond still sits on the throne. But that is about to change."

Change how? Maeve bit her tongue and pressed her lips tightly together. If she could somehow get the queen to disclose her plans, she might be able to use that information to her advantage.

"Ion." The queen gestured to Una's son. "Remove the rope from her neck."

With trembling hands the young man tried to untie the rope.

"Do you possess nothing but thumbs?" the queen demanded. "I said untie her!"

"I am trying, my lady," Ion said.

Maeve's heart went out to him. She knew well what it was to be badgered and belittled. She offered him an encouraging smile. "The knot will come."

He didn't reply or even look at her, and Maeve said nothing more to distract him. To avoid the queen's wrath he needed to remove the rope quickly. The sweat rolled down his face as he concentrated on the task.

"Can you do nothing right?" Una began stomping across the Great Hall. But the rope fell away before she reached him.

The queen waved Ion away with her hand and smiled malevolently at Maeve. "Now where were we?"

"You were about to explain how you planned

to free King Owen and depose King Redmond," Maeve said.

For a moment the queen raised an eyebrow in surprise, but then she laughed. "You have the look of your mother, but you are eminently more wily." Queen Ailsa became stone-faced once more. "You are your father's daughter as well."

The ring on Maeve's thumb tightened, and it took all Maeve's will not to glance down at it. Her heart was pounding and her mind was spinning with questions. She almost opened her mouth to give voice to them when the crystal at her throat began to pulse with soothing warmth. Maeve's heart slowed, her muscles relaxed and she once more took charge of her emotions.

Keeping her face expressionless, she stared at Queen Ailsa. Maeve could tell she was waiting for her to react. When she didn't, the queen's expression became iron.

"Ciara is dead so she cannot see you die," she said. "That is a pity because it is my pain I wish to see matched. Your sister is with child. The death of her babe will provide the same grief I think, and that will suffice."

"No," Maeve protested. "You cannot. Deirdre has done nothing to you. She is not even my blood."

"Perhaps not," the queen said, "but you care for her. When her child is born, you will see its short life snuffed out. And your heart will twist with the pain of it. Even beyond the grave, Ciara will grieve with you. I grant it is not equal to losing her own child, which is why your death will follow the child's."

"But my sister is innocent in all this!" Maeve argued. "As is her child."

The queen shrugged. "It matters not. I have waited a long time, and I will have my revenge. A child for a child."

There was another flash of lightning, and in the sudden brightening of the room the queen's face shone with manic pleasure.

"It won't change your situation, nor will it give you the satisfaction you desire." Maeve tried to reason with her.

"We shall see," the queen replied. "But the time for that has not yet arrived. In the meantime, allow me to make you welcome. After all, you are my guest." She nodded to Una's son. "Ion will escort you to your quarters."

The young man jumped into action. As he led Maeve from the Great Hall, the queen called after him, "See to it that our guest has everything she needs. Then remain outside in the hallway."

Ion turned and bowed. "Yes, my lady queen."

"Oh—and Ion," the queen said with scorn in her voice, "be sure to lock the door."

Chapter 19

As Maeve followed Ion down the stairs to the lower floor, her thoughts buzzed like riled bees.

The queen was mad. She was blinded by hate and there was no reasoning with her. Maeve must find a way to foil her plan, or she and Deirdre's baby were going to die. She could already feel her sister's despair. How such a thing could bring the queen pleasure, Maeve would never understand if she lived to be as old as Bradan, which seemed unlikely at this point.

Though she still hoped someone would be searching for her, she couldn't rely on being rescued. She needed to escape and find Deirdre. As far as she could tell, there were only three people to get past—the queen, Una and Ion. The odds weren't in Maeve's favour, but they weren't terrible either. The queen and Una were dangerous, but Ion seemed less of a threat. He did everything the queen and his mother commanded, but he struck Maeve as an unwilling villain. She felt more sorry for him than fearful.

"Thank you for not tugging on the rope," she said as they began their walk along the lower hallway. "I have been tethered for many days and my neck is raw."

He glanced back at her and nodded.

Encouraged, Maeve spoke again. "It is fortunate for the queen that the castle has a secret entrance."

"The castle has many secrets," he mumbled. "Cubbyholes and chambers—passageways too."

Maeve didn't ask how he knew that. Like as not he'd taken refuge in them to avoid torment.

"I shouldn't have said that," he blurted, a hint of panic in his voice and a fresh film of sweat on his brow. "If they knew I had told you, they would be angry."

"I have no reason to speak of it to them," Maeve assured him.

Ion pointed to the door by the table and chair. "This is your chamber."

More like my prison cell, Maeve thought but said nothing.

Ion stuck the torch into a sconce on the wall, lifted a ring of keys from an iron peg and unlocked the door. "If you need anything, knock." He nodded to the chair. "I shall be here." Then he pushed open the door and gestured for Maeve to go in. As soon as she did, the door closed behind her and the key turned in the lock.

The room was neither large nor small—merely dark. The only light came from a small fire in the grate on the wall adjacent to the door. A modest stack of wood lay nearby. The sight of a window on the outer wall set Maeve's thoughts racing. A window might offer a means of escape. This lower level of Castle Carrick was probably not far above ground, and though it wasn't a large window, Maeve wasn't a large person. A seed of optimism took root in her. She noted a table with a cup, a ewer of water and a plate of food. She looked beyond it to the far end of the chamber. It was dark, but Maeve thought she would find a sleeping pallet there. As she looked, she detected something in the shadows.

It moved. Maeve froze. She wasn't alone. Should she bang on the door for Ion? What if he wasn't there or was slow to respond? What if whoever was here attacked her before she got to the door?

"Who is here?" she demanded as boldly as she could manage.

There was no reply.

"Show yourself," she called again, hoping her bravado would scare the intruder.

"Maeve?" a timid voice ventured. "Is that you?"

"Deirdre?"

"Oh, sister!" Deirdre burst from the shadows and threw her arms around Maeve. "Thank goodness it is you! I have been so afraid." She hugged Maeve hard.

Maeve was relieved beyond belief to know her sister was safe. Deirdre was a prisoner, but at least Maeve didn't have to search for her. They were together, and that was a great comfort.

Deirdre released Maeve from her hug and stepped back. “Have you been taken too? Or have you come to free me?”

“Both,” Maeve replied grimly.

“That makes no sense,” Deirdre said, sounding more like the sister Maeve remembered. “Speak plainly.”

“It’s a long story.”

“Then you’d best begin telling it. I don’t know where I am or why I was brought here.”

“You are in Castle Carrick of Meath in the Midlands,” Maeve said.

“You know this place?”

Maeve nodded. “There was a council of war here before the attack of the Norsemen. I came with the Druid, Bradan, who is an advisor to King Redmond.”

Even in the faint light of the fire, Maeve could see her sister’s eyes grow round. “I thought Druids were woodsy folk. You keep company with kings now?”

Maeve shook her head. “Not really. Bradan is my teacher, and his counsel is much sought after. He took me with him so I might learn. That is all.”

Deirdre frowned. “But why are you here now?”

So the queen can kill me, Maeve thought, though she said nothing.

“And why have I been brought here?” Deirdre demanded. “If you know, you must tell me.”

Maeve took Deirdre’s hand and led her to the pallet. “Sit.”

When she had, Maeve dropped down beside her. "As I said, it's a long story."

Maeve told Deirdre about Ciara and the queen's vow to kill her. She explained how Ciara had died while trying to flee from the queen's henchmen and how her child had lived.

"That is terrible," Deirdre said, "but what does it have to do with us?"

Maeve closed her eyes. It was not a story she wished to tell.

"Maeve?"

Maeve opened her eyes and looked into Deirdre's. "I was that child."

Confusion contorted Deirdre's face and she shook her head fiercely. "No. You were not. You could not be. We are sisters."

"Yes," Maeve assured her. "We are sisters—in our hearts, though we share no blood."

As she explained how Bronagh's baby had been stillborn and the exchange had been made, the expression on Deirdre's face became more and more stricken.

"You are an imposter!" she cried when Maeve had finished.

"Through no fault of my own!" Maeve protested. "I knew not who I was any more than you did." She didn't add that she would have left the home of the blacksmith and his cruel wife many beatings ago had she known the truth.

"That still doesn't explain why you are here now."

"The queen saw me at the council of war. Apparently I am much like my mother, and she immediately recognized Ciara in me. Once more the queen's ire was piqued and her desire for revenge was keen. She has already had one of her servants try twice to kill me." Maeve shrugged. "And now that she has escaped imprisonment by the Great King, she is about to try again."

"She has escaped?"

Maeve was puzzled. "You didn't know?"

Deirdre frowned. "Why would I?"

"Because she is here at Castle Carrick. Has she not spoken to you?"

"No," Deirdre said. She pushed herself to her feet and began to pace. "You are starting to frighten me, sister. How can you be so calm? You are a prisoner. I am a prisoner." She spun toward Maeve. "You still haven't told me why I am here. Was I used as bait to draw you out?"

Maeve couldn't bring herself to answer. She looked away.

"So I am to die as well?" Deirdre asked.

Maeve shook her head. "No. Not you." As she looked up at Deirdre, her eyes filled with tears. "A child for a child."

At first Deirdre looked confused, but as the meaning of Maeve's words sank in, she fell back a step.

Maeve jumped up from the pallet and hurried to her. "I know it's unthinkable, sister. But we won't let it happen. There is time before your child is born—at least another month. And if we don't find our own escape before then, someone will come for us. We have to be strong and keep our wits about us. The queen has not yet won."

Deirdre pushed Maeve away. "This is your fault. Because of you, my child is going to die!" She collapsed on the pallet and began to sob.

Maeve tried again to comfort her, but all her efforts were for naught. Though she wanted to deny her sister's accusation, she felt the guilt of it. What Deirdre said was true. She and her child had been dragged into the queen's vile plot because of Maeve.

"Deirdre, please," she pleaded. "You must try to stay calm. Being upset can't be good for your baby."

"How can I not be upset! And what do you care!" Deirdre screamed. "I never—" She froze in mid-sentence and clutched her belly.

Maeve immediately became anxious. "Deirdre? What's the matter?" She put her arm around her sister, and this time Deirdre didn't push her away. "Are you all right?"

"It's the baby," Deirdre whimpered, turning terrified eyes on Maeve. "It's coming. But it's too soon. It can't be born now."

"We shall find a solution," Maeve told Deirdre once she'd made her as comfortable as she could. Deirdre's pains were still far apart, which Maeve hoped meant they had time to devise a plan. "We must keep our wits about us and not panic."

Maeve was trying to remain calm for Deirdre's sake, but secretly she was terrified. Her sister was about to have her baby, and it was up to Maeve to help deliver it. Nora had tried to prepare her for the task, but that didn't mean she was ready, especially since the child was coming earlier than it should. Maeve knew that sometimes happened, and though the babe might be smaller, it could still be healthy. Though considering the queen's plans, that might not even matter.

A wave of despair threatened to swamp her. She was but one person. How could she deliver a baby and save them all from the queen? It seemed impossible.

"What are we going to do?"

The fear in Deirdre's voice jolted Maeve back into the moment. She must be strong for her sister.

Maeve dabbed Deirdre's brow with a cloth torn from her shift and dampened with water from the ewer. She hoped that would provide some comfort. "Ssshhh. You are strong and you must be brave for your child." Maeve tried to remember the things Nora had told her about birthing. "Take deep breaths," she said.

Deirdre's body stiffened. Her pains were getting closer. Nora had said the birth might take many hours, but Deirdre's child seemed impatient to be born, and Maeve feared they didn't have much time. She had to prepare for the child's arrival.

"I must speak with our guard," she said. "There are things needed for the birth."

Deirdre gripped Maeve's arm. Her eyes were wild with fear. "No, sister. You must not. He can't know the baby is coming. He'll tell the queen!"

Maeve shook her head. "I don't think so. I have reason to believe he will help us. Even if he doesn't, we will be no worse off than we are now." She paused. "He is our only hope."

Deirdre clung to Maeve's arm. "No. You mustn't. I beg you."

Maeve had a thought, and looking into her sister's worried face, she smiled encouragingly. "I am a seer," she said. "You know that."

"Yes." Deirdre was wary. "How is that a help?"

"I have seen you with your child—more than once," Maeve insisted. It was true. She had seen Deirdre with her baby. This made Maeve more determined than ever to give her sister hope. "I would not have seen you thus if your child was going to be taken from you."

"Why should I believe you?" Deirdre searched Maeve's face as if she might find the truth there.

"Because I would not lie. I had a vision of you with your child once before I knew I was a seer and then again after I'd started my apprenticeship. I do not yet know how we are going to escape the queen, but we shall." Please let that be true, she added to herself.

Chapter 20

Maeve rapped on the door and listened for the sound of the key in the lock.

Ion cautiously entered the room. "What do you want?"

"We need clean cloths and a candle," she said. "And more water."

"Why?" His eyes narrowed.

Deirdre let out a loud moan.

"What is the matter with her?" he demanded, stepping farther into the chamber and nodding toward the pallet. "Is she ill?"

"Her baby is coming," Maeve said. There was no point in lying. The truth would be plain soon enough.

Beads of sweat broke out on Ion's brow. "I-I-I must tell the queen."

Maeve put a hand on his arm, and he pulled back. She dropped her hand. "Please, no. I beg of you, Ion. Do not tell the queen. This child won't be born for many hours. My sister has done Queen Ailsa no harm. Let her birth this baby in peace."

Ion looked past Maeve into the darkness where Deirdre lay. She cried out again and he flinched.

"Please, Ion," Maeve pleaded. "Where is the harm in granting my request? My sister and I are locked in this chamber. Even if the queen learns the child is coming, she will do nothing until it is born."

He shook his head. "I cannot help you. It is too dangerous. You don't know the queen. If she thinks I have disobeyed her, she will have me beaten and thrown into the dungeon. It has happened before."

"But I do know the queen," Maeve countered. "Perhaps better than you do. She murdered my mother, and now she wants to kill me and my sister's child. Would you help her in that effort? Because if you tell her the child is coming, that's what you'll be doing. Could you live with yourself knowing you had helped kill me"—she paused and glanced toward the pallet where Deirdre lay—"and an innocent babe? All I ask is that my sister be allowed this brief time with her child. You can say you weren't aware the child was coming. Men have no sense of such matters."

"She will know I'm lying. She always does," he insisted, backing toward the door. "And she will beat me."

"But she won't kill you," Maeve said. She could see he was wavering. "Please, Ion. We need your help."

Biting his lip and cowering like a cornered animal, he backed out of the room. "I will try," he mumbled as he pulled the door shut.

Maeve could only hope that Ion would find the courage to do as she'd asked. She poked at the dwindling fire and threw on another log. There was just one more left. When Ion came back she would ask him to bring more.

Deirdre groaned. Judging from the intensity and closeness of her pains, Maeve worried they were running out of time. Ion should have returned by now. How long could it take to find cloth and a candle? She needed those supplies.

She hurried back to Deirdre.

"The pains are stronger," her sister panted, pushing herself up onto her elbows. She was drenched with sweat.

Maeve wet the cloth and patted her face and neck. "Do you want to sit up?"

Deirdre shook her head. "I fear I would fall over." She smiled. Then her expression sobered. "Sister, I am sorry for what I said. I know that you are trying to help me. I am grateful that you are here and—" She grimaced as another pain took her. When it had passed, she added, "My husband's family knows I am missing. Help will come. Fergus will search for me. I'm sure of it."

Maeve smiled and patted Deirdre's hand. Her sister was trying to be brave, and Maeve was glad of it. But she would have felt more confident if they had a plan.

She heard the key turn in the lock. "Finally!" she exclaimed, jumping up from the pallet. But before she could take a step toward the door, it swung open and Una swept into the room. Close behind was Ion, looking as defeated as a whipped dog.

Maeve froze, her body shielding her sister.

"I understand the child is on its way." Una's lips stretched into a mocking smile. She looked past Maeve but ventured no closer. "That is splendid news. The queen will be pleased."

Maeve wanted to rush forward and slap the smug expression off Una's face, but the warm pulsing of the crystal at her throat kept her where she was. "The child will come in its own time. First babies are in no hurry to be born," she said with an authority she neither possessed nor felt. "The queen will have to wait."

Una's smile shrivelled. "I shall enjoy watching you die," she said.

"I imagine you would, should it come to that," Maeve said with a shrug. "In any case, I expect the queen will see to it herself. You would only bungle things—again."

Hatred flared in Una's eyes, and her hands became fists.

"I asked Ion for supplies," Maeve said.

Una pulled her son from behind her and pushed him roughly toward Maeve. "Give them to her," she barked.

Ion stumbled across the room, mouthing the words, I'm sorry. A red handprint branded his cheek. As he gave Maeve the cloths and candle, he said in a whisper, "She caught me." And then he scuttled back to his mother.

Una glowered at him before turning her attention back to Maeve. "When the child is born, Ion will bring the two of you to the Great Hall to be presented to the queen."

Deirdre gasped and grabbed the back of Maeve's robe. Maeve reached behind and placed her hand over her sister's.

Presented to the queen? Una made it sound like they were being invited to a celebration—not their execution. She knew she should be afraid, but there was no time for that. She had to help Deirdre birth her baby, and she had to come up with a plan to keep the child—and herself—alive.

The door closed just as Deirdre was taken by another pain. Maeve went to the fire, lit the candle and then hurried back to Deirdre and bathed her face and neck with cool water.

"The babe is coming," Deirdre panted.

Maeve tore a strip of cloth, rolled it tightly and told her sister to bite on it. "It will muffle your cries," she said. "We don't want Ion to suspect the child is born."

Deirdre nodded.

It was time. Maeve's heart skipped several beats. Nora had said Deirdre and the baby would do the bulk of the work, but she could help. She reminded herself of Nora's instructions. Then she checked her supplies. She had everything that would be needed. She took a deep breath. They could do this. As Deirdre was taken by another pain, Maeve squeezed her hand. “Push.”

Maeve’s heart swelled with joy as she looked upon her sister with her new son. He was tiny but perfect. Never had she witnessed such love. It was exactly as she had seen it in her mind.

And yet Maeve was uneasy. Though the sight of Deirdre and her child matched her vision, it did not prove they could defeat the queen. And despite her assurances to Deirdre that all would be well, Maeve still had no plan.

She had to get Deirdre and the child to safety. But how? She would have to enlist Ion’s help. The young man obeyed the queen and his mother out of fear. Somehow Maeve must convince him to help her instead.

As she pondered the best way to proceed, awareness of her surroundings dimmed. So when the door of the chamber burst open and Ion stumbled in, she was caught completely by surprise. Unable to keep his feet, he sprawled awkwardly onto the floor. Maeve gasped—not because of the nature of his entrance, but because of the dripping wet figure who stomped in after him.

“Fergus!” Deirdre cried. “Fergus, you found me!”

Hearing his name, Fergus abandoned his assault on Ion.

"Deirdre? Is that you?" he said as he bolted past Maeve.

Deirdre had been right. Fergus had come for her. Maeve moved to shut the door so that Ion couldn't run out to the queen, but another figure entered the chamber before she got there. He was wrapped in a sodden mantle, the hood draped over his head. Likely a friend of Fergus, Maeve thought. She breathed easier, knowing their numbers were growing. The stranger locked the door from the inside and then turned toward her.

Maeve blinked several times to make sure her eyes weren't deceiving her. She tried to speak but she had no voice.

Then a drenched Declan swept her into a huge wet hug.

"Praise Taranis," he murmured into her hair. "I was so afraid something terrible had befallen you."

Maeve felt herself melt. Declan was here, which meant the burden of escape no longer lay solely with her. She still didn't know how they would manage it, but she now felt confident they would.

"I dared not hope you would find me." She gestured toward the pallet and amended her declaration. "Find us. Deirdre has given birth—a fine boy. But as soon as the queen learns he is born, she will kill him."

"We shall be gone from this place long before that happens." Declan released her and turned to Ion. "Who is this? If he is a guard, he is a poor one.

He was asleep outside the door. It was a small matter to overpower him and let ourselves in."

Ion cowered in the corner.

"His name is Ion," Maeve said. "He is the son of the queen's woman." Then she lowered her voice so only Declan could hear. "He has been gentle and kind with me. We needn't fear him."

Declan looked unsure. He pulled the chair away from the table and pointed to it. "Sit," he barked, and when the young man had done so, he added, "And don't move. My friend has no liking for you."

"How did you find us?" Maeve asked. "How did you get into the castle?"

"It is a long story we don't have time for now. We must get away from here."

Lightning flashed and thunder boomed. Maeve shook her head. "We can't. Not now. The storm is too terrible. Deirdre isn't strong enough to travel, and her babe will not survive the cold and rain. Even if we could escape, we have nowhere to go."

"We can hide in the castle," Deirdre called from the darkness. "It is a large fortress."

"And the queen knows every corner of it," Ion grumbled. All eyes turned to him. "She would find you. Believe me."

"Well, we can't stay here," Deirdre persisted. "It is only a matter of time until she sends that Una woman to check on us."

"Or does so herself," Maeve muttered. "But you're right, Deirdre—we can't stay where we are." She spun toward Ion. "You said there were secret chambers and passages in the castle. You know where they are. We can hide in one of those. The queen wouldn't think to look for us there."

Ion scowled and shook his head. "Do you have any idea what she—and my mother," he added with a shudder, "would do to me if you escaped while I was guarding you?"

Maeve had her suspicions. "You could come with us," she said. "If they can't find you, they can't hurt you."

Lightning lit up the room once more and was followed immediately by another clap of thunder.

Ion flinched. "The storm is getting worse. The queen is no fool. She knows you wouldn't venture out in it. If I disappeared with you, she would comb the secret rooms and passages until she found us."

Fergus jumped up from the pallet. "Why are you asking this wretch for help? He is one of them. He would run to the queen the second he'd hidden us. We'd be more trapped than we are now."

"Fergus is right," Declan said with finality. "The fellow can't be trusted. We'll find our own escape. We'll tie him up, lock him in here and take the keys with us. The queen might not discover we're gone until morning."

"That's all well and good," Maeve retorted, "except for the small detail that we have nowhere to go. We cannot chase around the castle trying to avoid capture." She gestured toward Deirdre and the baby. "It would be too hard on them."

"Then what do you suggest?" Declan asked with obvious irritation. "We can't stay here, and we certainly can't let this fellow go free. He'll run straight for the queen. But if we keep him here too long, his mother will come to check on things."

And then she'll want to take us to the queen. "That's it!" Maeve cried, drawing all eyes to her.

"What's it?" Declan said. "You have a plan?"

Maeve's eyes sparkled as she bobbed her head. "I think so. What if, instead of running from the queen, we run to her?"

Declan pulled back and regarded Maeve skeptically. "That makes no sense."

She grinned. "Hear me out." She explained her idea, and when she was done she spun toward Ion. "Will you help us?"

The young man looked terrified. "It is too dangerous. The queen will kill me. You know s-s-she will."

Maeve shook her head. "Not if we succeed."

With the rope once more tied around her neck, Maeve trailed Ion up the tower stairs, fiercely hugging the wrapped bundle in her arms. It was no use running from the queen. Even if Maeve managed to escape with Deirdre's child, the queen would find them again. As long as Queen Ailsa remained free, they would never be safe.

Their only hope was to recapture her. Numbers were on their side—they were now five against two. The queen didn't know about Fergus and Declan, nor did she know that Ion had turned against her. Maeve prayed his new-found courage would hold up under the pressure that lay ahead. Surprise was in their favour, and they must make the most of it. They had a basic plan, but they would have to improvise as they went. Maeve was confident they could succeed, but they still needed to be wary of the queen.

As they exited the staircase onto the main floor of the castle, Maeve glanced over her shoulder. From several paces back, Declan nodded encouragement. She took a deep breath and followed Ion through the main foyer to the Great Hall. Just inside the entrance she stopped. The fire had been refreshed and burned brightly, casting more light. Candles had been lit as well. The queen was on her throne and Una stood beside her, head bent, listening attentively to her mistress.

"My lady queen," Ion called. His voice shook. Maeve felt a prickle of concern. Ion lived in perpetual anxiety, but this night he had more cause than usual. Hopefully the queen and Una wouldn't notice.

They looked up.

"The child is b-born," Ion stammered. "A boy. I have brought it and the Druid girl to you as-as you requested."

"It was a command, you fool—not a request," his mother growled.

"Now, now, Una, don't be so hard on the boy,"

the queen purred. "He has done well—for a change." She curled a finger, beckoning him. "Come closer. I wish to see this child."

Ion started forward, but Maeve stood firm and the rope stretched taut.

"I said bring the child to me," the queen said, the silkiness gone from her voice.

"She resists," Ion said, dragging a sleeve across his perspiring brow. "She will not come."

"Then take the child from her, you fool!" his mother shouted.

"If you want this child, Queen Ailsa," Maeve called, "you will have to tear it from my arms. I shall not give it up willingly."

"As you wish." The queen sneered, pushing herself to her feet and moving to a nearby table. She picked up a jewel-handled dagger and watched the blade flash in the firelight. Then she glided back to her throne and pressed the knife into Una's hand. "Bring me the child. Use the dagger if need be, but do not kill the girl. I wish to have that pleasure."

Una didn't waste a moment. She crossed the hall quickly, the dagger gripped menacingly in her hand. As she drew near, a flash of lightning blazed through the hall, fully illuminating the hatred she bore Maeve.

Ion stepped in front of her. "No, Mother," he said. "You cannot."

Una pushed him aside. "Get out of my way! I shall deal with you later." She made a grab for the bundle in Maeve's arms, but Maeve pulled away, beyond her reach.

"As you wish," Una snarled, raising the dagger.

But before she could strike, Ion leaped forward, wrapped an arm tightly around his mother's neck and knocked the dagger from her hand.

"Let me go!" Una screeched. "You stupid boy!"

"Stop struggling, Mother," Ion said. "I do not wish to hurt you." Dragging his flailing mother with him, he backed away so Maeve had a clear view of the queen.

She nodded her gratitude before turning to Queen Ailsa. "It would appear it is just you, me and the child." She was aware that her cockiness would rile the queen, and she steeled herself for the attack she knew would come. She reminded herself she wasn't alone. Declan was only a few steps away.

The queen started toward her. She was smiling. "You can't best me with a child in your arms," she said. "Nor can you outrun me." She bent down and picked up the dagger from the floor. Then she continued gliding toward Maeve. "Give me the child. I won't ask again."

Maeve glanced at the bundle in her arms. Gently shifting it, she held it out with two hands. The queen smiled victoriously and stepped closer, but as soon as she reached for the bundle, Maeve heaved it with all her might at the queen's head. It struck her full in the face and then fell to the floor, rolling free of its swaddling.

The queen staggered, dropped the dagger, and clutched at her face. Declan jumped out from his hiding place and pounced on her, binding her hands before she could regain her senses. Maeve removed the rope from her own neck and tied it around the queen's. Then she fetched the rope Declan had left in the main foyer and helped Ion tie up his mother.

When both the queen and Una were securely bound, Declan retrieved the log that had served as the baby in Maeve's arms and tossed it on the fire. Then he picked up the cloth that had swaddled it and handed it to Ion. He nodded toward Una, who was screeching like an enraged banshee.

Ion made his way slowly across the room and, for a long moment, did nothing but stare down at his mother while she continued to gabble angrily. Finally he said, "Rest your voice, Ma," and stuffed the wadded cloth into her mouth.

Chapter 21

Until King Redmond could be informed of the queen's capture, she and Una were locked in the chamber Maeve and Deirdre had shared. Initially Maeve had been worried they might try to escape through the window, but Ion assured her that was unlikely. The window was located on the western side of the castle, where the land fell into a deep ravine.

Ion seemed relieved to see the queen and her lady imprisoned, though he was still incredulous. "I can't quite believe it," he said with a shake of his head. "At any moment I expect them to burst from the chamber and whip me."

"No one is going to whip you ever again," Maeve assured him. "You were very brave, Ion, and I shall be forever grateful. You saved my sister's child—and me. We couldn't have done this without you."

The young man looked away shyly and nodded.

Ion was left to stand guard while the others returned to the Great Hall, but because he doubted his ability to resist the queen's commands and his mother's browbeating, he insisted they take the keys with them.

"I am in awe of you," Deirdre said to Maeve as the four young people sat before the fire. "If anyone was coming at me with a dagger, I'd have run off screaming."

"I was tempted, believe me," Maeve replied. She put a hand on Declan's arm. "But I knew Declan was nearby and would protect me."

"Was that what I was supposed to do?" Declan feigned surprise. "You should have told me."

Maeve laughed and swatted his arm. Then she sobered again and said, "How is it you and Fergus came here together, and how on earth did you know where to find us?"

"You tell the story, Fergus," Declan said. "You know it better than I."

Fergus nodded. "It was a fortunate coincidence," he said. "I was on my way back from the village, where I'd been looking for Deirdre, when a cart carrying two men passed me on the road. I didn't recognize them, but I was too beside myself with worry over Deirdre to give them any thought. Then I heard moaning in the trees, so I left the track to see what it was about. That's when I found Declan. He had a nasty bump on his head. He wasn't feeling too good, and that's for certain.

"As soon as he was able, he explained who he was and how the pair of you had been looking for Deirdre when he got hit on the head. Just before that, though, he said he'd heard you calling him and had looked up to see a fellow behind you. So we figured there must have been two men, and since you were nowhere about, they must have taken you. When we went looking to see if you'd left a clue behind, we found Deirdre's basket and signs of a struggle. We figured that wherever she'd been spirited away to is likely where you were being taken as well. That's when I remembered the cart that had passed me, so we decided to chase after it." Fergus gestured for Declan to take over the story.

"All I can think is that the fellows who took you must have been following us from the time we left the Ruin."

"With a cart?" Maeve objected. "How is that possible? We stayed away from the roads."

Declan shook his head. "I don't think they had the cart early on. It was likely a solution of convenience. Remember we saw a cart at Fergus's farm? There was a horse nearby too."

Maeve nodded. "I suppose."

"You'd think I'd have recognized my own horse and cart." Fergus shook his head.

Deirdre patted his arm. "You had other more important things on your mind."

"That's right." Declan nodded and continued with the story. "Anyway, when we got to the village we discovered the cart had passed through but hadn't stopped. The folk we talked to said it was following the road north. We needed to catch up to it, though we didn't want to stop it until it reached its destination in case you were being taken to the same place as Deirdre. Since we didn't know how long the journey would take, we bought supplies in the village and pushed on. The cart tracks were easy to follow and we caught up to it that night.

"It pained me to see you tethered," Declan said, turning soulful eyes on Maeve, "but if I'd tried to free you, we'd never have found Deirdre. You have to know I would never have let them harm you."

"I do," Maeve assured him. "I would never doubt you, Declan. And as much as I did not enjoy my journey, I'm glad you did what you did. It worked." Looking to Fergus, she steered the story back on track. "You were able to follow the cart without being seen until it arrived at Castle Carrick?"

"Is that where we are now?" Fergus asked, looking around.

"Yes."

He nodded. "We saw the men hand you over to that vile woman and watched as she and her lad took you into the castle through the secret entrance. But we had to bide our time before following because we were afraid they'd hear the rock move."

Declan shivered. "We were well and truly drenched by the time we got inside. Then we had to work out where they'd taken you without getting caught ourselves. We peeked into every cell in the dungeon. When we finally got to the next level, we saw Ion sitting in the hall. We were certain he was guarding one of you. So we watched and waited for our chance." He shrugged. "The rest you know."

Maeve turned to Deirdre. "Sister, how did you get here?"

Deirdre looked down at the babe in her arms. "Much the same as you, I expect. Not the same thugs, though. I'm sure the queen has many henchmen to do her dirty work.

"My kidnapper must have learned it is my habit to go to the village every morning, for he was waiting in the trees. He dragged me from the road, gagged me, tied my hands and placed a hood over my head. Then he forced me onto his horse and climbed up behind me." She shuddered and wrinkled her nose with distaste. "He was an unwashed scruff with onion breath.

"We stayed clear of the village and the roads, riding all day and most of the night. We arrived here about midday. The fellow stopped once to rest the horse and allow me to relieve myself. He gave me some water and a crust of bread. That was the only time I was without the hood. It wasn't until I was within the castle that it was removed for good."

Maeve frowned. "I imagine that was because it was not the queen's plan to kill you, and she didn't want you knowing where you were being taken."

Deirdre leaned her head on Fergus's shoulder. "Thank goodness it's over now and we're all safe."

The next day Ion escorted Declan to the local chieftain, who was informed of the queen's capture.

After that matters progressed rapidly. The chieftain had his soldiers move Una and Queen Ailsa to the dungeon in his fortress for safekeeping until King Redmond could send soldiers to collect them. The chieftan also provided a horse, cart and driver to see the young people safely home. And best of all, he found a job for Ion at his castle.

"I shall miss you, sister." Deirdre sniffed and wiped away a tear when it came time for Maeve and Declan to continue south on their own. Then she stomped her foot. "I hate this! Motherhood has turned me into a weeping fool."

Maeve laughed. "What is wrong with a few tears? You are not a block of wood. You are a caring woman who is going to make a fine mother. Baby Conn is a lucky little fellow."

The sisters hugged while Fergus and Declan clapped each other on the back.

"Good-bye, sister." Deirdre waved a final time as she climbed back into the cart.

"Good-bye, Deirdre. Good-bye, Fergus. Take care of baby Conn," Maeve called after them. "We shall see you again very soon."

Declan put an arm around Maeve. "Well, that was quite an adventure," he said. "I never know what to expect with you."

She grinned up at him. "Don't feel badly. Neither do I. And I'm a seer!"

Maeve was thankful to be back at the Ruin with Bradan and her friends, though she thought she would go mad if she had to tell the story of her encounter with the queen even one more time.

What she wanted more than anything was to talk to her mother. She needed to visit the Bridge of Whispers. But after three days she still hadn't found an opportunity to get away.

"Go," Bradan said when she begged to be freed from her lessons following the midday meal. "You have been through much. Go to the forest and find peace."

"Thank you, Bradan. You are wonderful!" She planted a kiss on his weathered forehead.

Bradan waved her away. "Off with you before I change my mind."

Maeve laughed and raced for the woods. As soon as she entered the trees, the restlessness that had been plaguing her floated away on the breeze. She spread her arms and gave herself up to the forest's embrace. She was home. Then, grinning for the sheer joy of it, she ran all the way to the bridge.

Standing in the middle, she looked down over the stone wall into the water.

"Mother?" she whispered. "Are you here?"

There was no reply and no reflection of Ciara in the stream. Maeve scanned the area, but there was no sign of her mother anywhere. And it wasn't just that Maeve couldn't see her; she couldn't feel her. No matter that she wanted with all her heart to speak to her. Ciara was not here.

A tear slid down her cheek. "Please don't abandon me, Mother," she pleaded into the air as she clutched the stone wall of the bridge.

Maeve continued to peer into the stream, searching for a sign of Ciara, though she knew her mother wouldn't be coming.

The crystal around her neck began to pulse with warmth, and Maeve pressed it hard to her heart.

She walked slowly back through the forest. She knew her mother would always be with her but not in the way she wanted. She had used her love to protect Maeve, but now the danger was past she had stepped back into the Otherworld. Maeve understood, but accepting was another matter.

When she reached the edge of the woods, she pushed her feelings of melancholy away. There was no sense wearing her sadness for all to see.

Pulling her shoulders back, she started into the meadow. Halfway across she spied a man walking south along the road toward the Ruin. He was leading a small donkey that put her in mind of Traveller. The thought of her friend lifted her spirits and she hurried to catch them up.

"Hello," she called and waved.

The man stopped and looked in her direction.

As did the donkey, and as soon as the creature saw Maeve, it brayed loudly, broke away from its master and began trotting toward her.

Maeve stopped and stared. This was very strange. As the animal got closer, her heart skipped a beat. Was it— She shook her head. No. It couldn't be. The donkey kept coming, with the man now chasing after him.

Maeve grinned. "Traveller?" she said, and the little donkey brayed again. "Traveller!" Maeve cried and started running too. "It is you!"

When the man caught up, Maeve was laughing and hugging the donkey, who was braying happily and nuzzling her pockets for treats.

"So you're to blame," the man puffed.

Maeve stopped laughing. "I'm so sorry," she apologized. "I didn't mean to make your donkey run away. It's just that we know each other. We are friends."

The man shook his head, but there was a glint in his eye as he said, "I'd say you're more than that. The beast has been mooning over you ever since Finn returned him to me. He does no work and he heads for the road leading back here every chance he gets." He shoved the lead into Maeve's hand. "A lovesick donkey is of no use to me."

Maeve stared stupidly at the rope. Then she frowned. "I don't understand. Are you giving me your donkey?"

He shrugged. "I can't see that I have a choice. Be sure you treat him well." And under his breath he added, "As if I need worry about that." He squinted through the sunlight toward the Ruin. "I've come a long way. A cup or two of ale wouldn't go amiss." And with that, he started back across the meadow shouting, "Finn, my friend, where be you? Me pipes are parched!"

Maeve joined Bradan in the arch of oak trees the following morning.

"Look up," Bradan said when she sat down. "What do you see?"

Maeve turned her gaze skyward. The branches of the oaks stretched upward, splayed like fingers grasping for the brilliant blue beyond, and the tip of each branch boasted a green bud.

Maeve looked back at Bradan and smiled. "I see spring."

Bradan smiled back. "And a welcome sight it is."

It amazed Maeve to think how much had happened in recent weeks. It seemed each day had brought a new discovery, delight, disappointment or danger. And it pleased her to see that as she had changed in the last few weeks, so had the trees.

They sat quietly for a few moments, breathing in the morning. Finally Bradan said, "Did you visit the Bridge of Whispers yesterday?"

Maeve stared into the distance and nodded.

"Ciara wasn't there?"

She shook her head.

He patted her hand. "She will be when you need her," he said kindly.

"I think I know that, but it still makes me sad that I can't see her whenever I would like."

"One day you will meet again," Bradan assured her. "In the meantime you have your life here. You have your friends, your gift—" He chuckled. "You even have the donkey."

Maeve smiled. She knew Bradan was right. She had much to be grateful for. "And when I need my spirits lifted, I have the forest," she said, trying to push past her melancholy.

"Ah, yes," Bradan said. "There's that. You are truly a child of the forest. But then you come by it honestly."

Maeve cocked her head. "Do I get that from my mother too?"

Bradan shook his head. "No. That is something you share with your father."

"My father," Maeve said as she unconsciously turned the silver ring on her thumb. "The queen spoke of him. She said he was wily and I was like him in that way."

Bradan's eyes crinkled at the corners. "Did she now?"

"Yes." Maeve nodded vigorously. "She did. Was he?"

It was several seconds before Bradan answered.

"Yes," he finally replied. "I suppose he was."

Maeve leaned toward the old Druid. "Tell me about him. Please."

As Bradan turned his gaze to the ring on Maeve's thumb, she could see him drifting back in time. It was all she could do not to press him to continue.

"Where to begin," he said at last. "Where to begin."

THE END

Dedication

In memory of my good friend, Paulette (1951 – 2020)
I'll meet you at the Bridge of Whispers

Acknowledgments

Behind every successful book is a cast of thousands. Okay, maybe I'm exaggerating a little, but there are a lot of people who contribute to a book. It starts with the writer of course, but once the story finds its way to paper or a computer screen, things start to move, and the people who are involved from that point on make all the difference. I don't know all their names or jobs, but I am grateful to each and every one of them.

I have great hopes for *The Bridge of Whispers*, thanks in large part to the uncompromising editing of Melanie Jeffs. We writers are not always objective, so it takes someone who can see the big picture to encourage the writer to dig deeper and flesh out the important stuff, to see what isn't there but should be, as well as point out what needs to go away. In the case of *The Bridge of Whispers*, there were 8,000 words that needed to go away. How Melanie managed to cut them without negatively affecting the story still has me shaking my head. In addition to Melanie's efforts, there were other eyes on the manuscript catching typos, house style inconsistencies, and problems with readability and clarity.

And what is a book without an intriguing cover? Many thanks to Rubén Carral Fajardo, who created this one. It perfectly captures the mood of the book. I couldn't be more pleased. And kudos to the designer, who finished it off and pulled the various parts of the book together to make a cohesive, attractive finished product.

Being the second book in *The Seer Trilogy*, it is important for *The Bridge of Whispers* to build on the first book. To that end, I would like to thank everyone who read *The Druid and the Dragon* and provided feedback and promotion of it on their websites and through word of mouth and social media. Also thanks to subscribers of *The Seer Trilogy* newsletter. I am grateful for your ongoing support and encouragement. It feels as if you are family. Thanks also to those who have taken the time to review *D&D,* and the booksellers who have promoted it in their shops. All of your efforts pave the way for this next book.

Thanks also to my writing group. The collective hive mind sees straight to the core of the work in progress and keeps me on course as I write.

Finally, I cannot overstate the importance of family and friends in this process. I regularly bombard my husband with story updates and pick his brain about such things as rubbing dirt on pitch to render it less sticky. He is also frequently asked to evaluate passages for clarity and credibility. Likewise my kids, especially my daughter, are asked their opinions about incidents in the story.

I have a wonderful support system. I couldn't ask for more. Thank you all.

ABOUT THE AUTHOR

Many writers are or have been teachers. Kristin Butcher is not quite sure why that is, but she is no exception. Kristin taught for twenty years–everything from primary science to high school English. She hadn't planned to be a teacher; it was something that happened while she wasn't looking. She hadn't planned to be a writer either. Writing is just something she's always done. She's been doing it professionally now for nearly twenty-five years, and she still loves it.